"So I Was Thinking, Bring Over Dinner Later Tonight?"

"Clay, it's not a good idea."

"I thought I had *good* ideas. You said so yourself about a dozen times last night."

His *ideas* had given her a night she'd never forget, but morning brought her sanity back. "Last night was incredible," she said honestly. "I'm not sorry, it's something we both wanted and needed, but we can't—"

"Why not? Why *can't* we?"

"Because it's pointless."

He hesitated for a moment. "Don't analyze it, Trish. We're still married."

For the next few weeks. "Well, I can't separate the two in my head. I can't make love with you and pretend we're not split up. I can't do that to myself or to Meggie. She's already lost so much."

"What is she going to lose if I come over for dinner?"

"It won't end there and you know it. While I'm here, I'm going to focus on the fundraiser. I won't have a lot of time for anything else."

Dubious, his eyes lit like sparks on the Fourth of July. "Count on me to change your mind."

* * *

Dear Reader,

Welcome back to glorious Red Ridge, Arizona, for Clayton Worth and Trisha Fontaine's story!

I'm thrilled to have *The Cowboy's Pride* be a part of the Billionaires and Babies series for Harlequin Desire this month. I promise you, not only will you fall in love with Clay, the sexy, onetime country music superstar now running Worth Ranch, but I'm pretty sure adorable, blond-haired, blue-eyed baby Meggie will steal your heart as well. She's a cutie!

I guess you could say, babies are my business, my *other* business. For the past twenty-five years, I've taught childbirth and baby-care classes to expectant parents. It's been a great honor and joy in my life. Creating Trish Fontaine's character, a new mommy who is learning parenting skills by the seat of her pants, has been truly fun.

The legend of Elizabeth Lake and the Worth family heirloom we see in *The Cowboy's Pride* story will be revealed when we step back in time to learn how Worth Ranch got its start. Coming in spring 2012 from Harlequin Historical and Charlene Sands, you'll meet Chance Worth and Lizzie Mitchell in 1884 Arizona!

Don't worry, I haven't forgotten about the third Worth brother. Jackson's story is coming soon, too!

Happy reading!

Charlene Sands

CHARLENE SANDS

THE COWBOY'S PRIDE

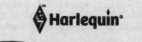

ISBN-13: 978-0-373-73140-4

THE COWBOY'S PRIDE

This edition published by arrangement with Harlequin Books S.A.

For questions and comments about the quality of this book please contact us at Customer_eCare@Harlequin.ca.

® and TM are trademarks of Harlequin Books S.A., used under license. Trademarks indicated with ® are registered in the United States Patent and Trademark Office, the Canadian Trade Marks Office and in other countries.

www.Harlequin.com

Printed in U.S.A.

Books by Charlene Sands

Harlequin Desire

Carrying the Rancher's Heir #2088
The Cowboy's Pride #2127

Silhouette Desire

The Heart of a Cowboy #1488
Expecting the Cowboy's Baby #1522
Like Lightning #1668
Heiress Beware #1729
Bunking Down with the Boss #1746
Fortune's Vengeful Groom #1783
Between the CEO's Sheets #1805
The Corporate Raider's Revenge #1848
*Five-Star Cowboy #1889
*Do Not Disturb Until Christmas #1906
*Reserved for the Tycoon #1924
Texan's Wedding-Night Wager #1964
†Million-Dollar Marriage Merger #2016
†Seduction on the CEO's Terms #2027
†The Billionaire's Baby Arrangement #2033

Historical

Lily Gets Her Man #554
Chase Wheeler's Woman #610
The Law and Kate Malone #646
Winning Jenna's Heart #662
The Courting of
  Widow Shaw #710
Renegade Wife #789
Abducted at the Altar #816
Bodine's Bounty #872
Taming the Texan #887
  "Springville Wife"
Western Weddings #895
  "Wearing the Rancher's Ring"
Western Winter
  Wedding Bells #1011

*Suite Secrets
†Napa Valley Vows

Other titles by this author available in ebook

CHARLENE SANDS

Award-winning author Charlene Sands writes bold, passionate, heart-stopping heroes and always…really good men! She's a lover of all things romantic, having married her high school sweetheart, Don. A member of the Romance Writers of America, she is the proud recipient of a Readers' Choice Award and double recipient of a Booksellers' Best Award, having written more than thirty romances to date.

When not writing, she loves movie dates with her hubby, playing cards with her children, reading romance, great coffee, Pacific beaches, country music and anything chocolate. She also loves to hear from her readers. You can reach Charlene at www.charlenesands.com or P.O. Box 4883, West Hills, CA 91308. You can find her on the Harlequin Desire Authors Blog, and on Facebook, too!

This story is dedicated to
all the sweet little babies in the world!

And to one very special baby girl, our first grandchild:

At the time of writing this dedication,
you haven't come out to greet us yet,
but you are precious and loved already!

One

The Arizona sky over Worth Ranch was cloudless blue, the air clear enough to view a distant yellow cab ambling up the road that led to the main house. A small cloud of crimson dust billowed up in the taxi's wake, before scattering to earth again.

"Looks like your wife's finally here," Wes said.

Clayton Worth followed the direction of his ranch foreman's gaze and gave a curt nod. He didn't have to tell him that Trisha Fontaine wasn't going to be his wife much longer. Everyone in Red Ridge knew their marriage was over.

"Cover your ears, Wes." Clay pulled off his leather work gloves and drew oxygen into his lungs. He shouldn't care so damn much that Trish was late getting here—by three days—he hadn't seen her for almost a year. "The fireworks are about to begin."

Wes Malloy sent him a halfhearted smile. "Breaking things off ain't ever easy, Clay."

His foreman had worked the ranch with Clay's father way back when, helping Rory Worth build his massive cattle empire. Nothing had mattered more to Rory than the family and the ranch. The two went hand in hand. Rory's dying plea had been for Clay to take over the reins at Worth Ranch and provide heirs to keep the family legacy strong.

But Clay hadn't been able to keep that vow to his father.

Not only had Trish refused him children, but she'd suspected him of betraying his marriage vows. Her accusation cut deep and when she'd walked out on him, it had been the last straw. If he'd had any doubts about the divorce, it vanished when he'd gotten Trish's voice mail message three days ago that something important had come up and she couldn't make the Penny's Song opening.

Something important was always coming up.

She should have been here. Despite their yearlong separation, the charity she helped him develop on Worth land for children recovering from illness should have meant more to her than that. He never thought she'd blow it off.

He'd been wrong.

Clay jammed his gloves into the back pockets of his Wranglers and took slow deliberate steps as he made his approach to the idling cab. He watched Trish get out of the backseat, stretching out her legs as she rose to her full height. Chest tight, Clay's breath caught and he recalled the first time he'd met her, the first time he'd seen those beautiful mile-high legs, backstage at a black-tie function in Nashville. Clay's country music superstardom had always brought big donors to charity events.

He'd bumped into her by accident—his big frame no match for her slender body. She toppled and he lunged for her just before she collided with the ground. He'd heard a rip from her too-tight dress and witnessed the gown split along the seam clear up to her thigh. Under the dim lights, her exposed skin glowed soft and creamy and something powerful happened to Clay then. Before he'd gotten her to a standing position, he asked her out to dinner. She'd refused him flat, but with a smile, and handed him her business card so he could make arrangements to pay for her ruined dress.

Hell, he never could resist a challenge *and* a beautiful woman.

But that was then.

"Trish." He stood a few feet from her.

"Hello, Clay," she said softly.

Unnerved by the breathy sound of her voice, he braced himself. It surprised him that she still could affect him that way. Trish's sighs and little gasps poured fire into his veins. That much hadn't changed. With a practiced eye, he skimmed over her body.

Half of her white blouse was out of the waistband of her pinstriped skirt. It hung along the side of her hip, haphazardly bunched. The tailored button-down blouse itself was travel-wrinkled, as she would say, stained by some mystery food and looking like it had seen better days. Long strands of her honey-blond hair stuck out of a cockeyed velvet bow in a bad attempt at a ponytail. Smudges of deep cherry-red lipstick colored the lower part of her chin.

In short, Trisha Fontaine Worth, his soon to be ex-wife, was a beautiful mess.

She caught his look of confusion. No one could ever say she was slow. "I know. Don't say it. I look like something the cat dragged in."

He was wise enough not to comment. "Bad trip?"

Trish shrugged. "Bad *everything* lately." She darted a quick glance inside the backseat of the cab and then spoke to the taxi driver, "Give me one minute, please."

When she faced him again, the weary tone of her voice bordered on apology. "I missed the opening of Penny's Song.

I tried reaching you a few times and well, I didn't want to explain it to your answering machine."

Clay had been piss angry with her for half a dozen reasons, but at the moment, he wasn't so much mad as he was curious. What the heck was up with her? He'd never seen Trish look so...scattered. What happened to the ever capable, well-organized and fashion-conscious woman who'd stolen his heart three years ago?

"I never thought you'd miss it, Trish." They'd caused each other injury and frustration, but the one thing they'd always agreed upon, the one thing that rose above their personal trials, had been the founding of Penny's Song.

"Neither did I, and believe me, I tried to—"

He heard little whimpers coming from inside the cab. The sound brought him up short. "What's that? Don't tell me you got a *dog*."

Her eyes widened. She whirled around so fast that he nearly missed it when he blinked. "Oh! It's the baby. She's waking up."

Baby?

But by that time, Trish had already reached inside the backseat of the cab.

When she reemerged, she was gently shushing a baby wrapped in a delicate pink blanket. Hips swaying, she took careful steps, rocking the bundle in her arms with a soft smile. Clay noted her entire demeanor changed the minute she'd lifted the baby. "It's okay, sweet baby. It's okay." She spared Clay a glance and offered, "She fell asleep in the car seat."

Clay stepped forward. He'd been focused solely on Trish. He hadn't noticed a car seat in the cab or anything else for that matter. He peeked over the blanket, taking in the baby's honey-wheat blond hair and crystal blue eyes. The same shade as Trish's. A tick worked at his jaw. He didn't know much about babies, but he sure as hell knew that the child was at least four months old. Trish had left him one year ago. Doing the math wasn't rocket science.

His heart pounded against his chest. "Whose baby is that?"

Trish snapped her eyes to his and began shaking her head. "Oh no, Clay…it's not what you think. The baby's not yours."

Clay blinked and rocked back on his heels. The implication was there, out in the open, and his gut clenched with the knowledge. He tried a deep breath to steady his rising temper.

For the sixteen years Clay had been in country music, women had flung themselves at him nearly every day. He'd fended off groupies by the dozens. There were always rumors hard to live down, but once he'd met Trish, he'd made it publicly known he was attached and planned on staying that way. He'd never betrayed her. Not during those days when he traveled on the country circuit and not now as he ran the Worth empire. Even throughout their separation, he'd been faithful to his vows.

And damn it, he'd expected the same from her. "But she's *yours?*"

She nodded, sending him a look of deep regret. "Yes, she's mine."

Clay let out a string of curses that would shock his poker buddies. He didn't know which news troubled him the worst. That the child was his and she'd kept it from him, or that the baby wasn't his, which meant she'd cheated on him during their time apart.

"You got pregnant?"

Color drained from her face and her eyes filled with pain.

What was with her anyway? Did she think that showing up here with a baby that wasn't his wouldn't rile him? Did she think that he would welcome her and accept them both without question? The divorce she came for today couldn't happen soon enough for him now.

"No, Clay. I didn't get pregnant." She acted like the idea was absurd and that he was a jerk to even think it. Her voice trembled with indignation. "There...there hasn't been anyone else."

Her earnest admission split his anger in half. He narrowed his eyes staring at her expression, remembering one thing about his wife. She wasn't a liar. He *believed* her. Relief raced through his body. He wasn't sure why his heart tripped hearing her declaration. Or why he'd felt like a weight had been lifted from his shoulders. He shouldn't feel like doing a tap dance because his estranged wife hadn't cheated on him.

He tipped his hat farther back on his forehead, trying to make sense of it all. Determined to get to the truth, he folded his arms across his chest and eyed her carefully. "I'm still waiting for that explanation."

Trish inhaled deeply. Her eyes softened when she glanced at the child in her arms. "I'm adopting her."

Adopting her?

Clay blinked and shook the cobwebs out of his head. Wasn't this the woman who'd told him over and over that she wasn't ready for motherhood? The woman who'd told him she needed more time, until the waiting seemed like it would never end. Wasn't this the woman who'd caused him to break his vow to his dying father?

"What?"

She turned sideways to shield the baby from the afternoon sun and looked at him over her shoulder. "Clay, can we talk inside the house? Meggie's squinting. And I'm pretty sure she shouldn't be out in this heat."

That was the first thing she'd said during their conversation that made any sense. Clay gestured with a nod toward the house. "The door's unlocked. Take the baby and go on inside. I'll deal with the cabdriver and your things and I'll be back in a few minutes."

"Thank you. Oh, and Clay, there's a lot of *things*." Trish nibbled on her lower lip. "Babies, I'm learning, come with their own set of gear."

Trish heard Clay speaking with the cabdriver as she held Meggie tight to her chest and walked along the path where flower beds of white and yellow lilies and purple hyacinth thrived. Everything looked the same as she remembered. With its wraparound veranda supported by polished wood railings and centered by a wide double door, the spacious two-story ranch house embodied old Southwest charm. The first time Clay had brought her here, she'd been awestruck by the expanse and splendor of Worth land and the surrounding Red Ridge Mountains, but she'd been even more enamored of Clay, the man she'd eventually wed.

She'd planned on having his children, one day. She'd discussed it with Clay in obscure terms for the most part before they'd married. But then Clay's father passed and suddenly her husband was hell bent on having a baby.

Right away.

His sudden change in plans had floored her. She hadn't been ready for motherhood back then. Heck, she wasn't ready for it now. The thought of screwing up something as important as raising a child struck fear in her heart. She didn't want to make the same mistakes her mother had made. But Meggie had come into her life and Trish wouldn't let her down.

On a deep breath, she turned the doorknob and opened the front door. A wave of nostalgia hit her as she stepped inside the house. "Oh, Meggie," she whispered.

She'd lived in this house with Clay and they'd been happy once. Tears welled in her eyes. She'd missed living on the ranch, but she didn't know just how much until she stepped over the threshold. She stood there a minute, as sensations flooded her. She and Clay had started a life here, a *good* life, but obstacles had gotten in the way and as much as he would lay the blame on her, her stubborn soon-to-be ex had played a hand in their breakup.

Clay's part-time housekeeper approached the foyer and greeted her with a cautious smile. "Mrs. Worth, it's good to see you. Welcome home." Her gaze went straight to the baby.

"Hello, Helen. I'm glad to see you, too." But she wasn't really *home*. After her brief stay, she'd have no place here anymore. "I'll be living at the guesthouse while I'm here, but I—"

"Yes, Clayton has told me. I've got everything set for you in there. But, oh my, I wasn't expecting—"

"I know. Neither was I. This is Meggie," Trish said, turning slightly to show her the baby's face. "Isn't she sweet?"

Helen's eyes softened and she touched the baby blanket gently just under Meggie's chin. "She's a beautiful baby."

"I think so, too." Trish brushed a kiss to Meggie's forehead. The poor child. She had no idea what was happening. They'd traveled across the country to get here, a trip that had taken its toll on both of them.

Helen waited a split second for more explanation, but Trish held her tongue. Clay's housekeeper had a momma bear protective streak when it came to the Worth men, and Trish already suspected she wasn't in her good graces for walking out on Clay and moving back to Nashville. Of course, she doubted Helen knew all the details and she wouldn't hear them from her.

"Would you like something to drink?" Helen asked. "I've got a pot of coffee still on."

"No, thank you. I think we're just going to sit down in the parlor and wait for Clay."

Helen nodded and then looked Trish over as if just noticing her state of dishevelment. "If I can do anything for you, let me know."

How about a course in Motherhood 101? Trish could write a book about what she didn't know about raising a baby. Every spare moment she'd managed this month had been spent poring over parenting books.

"I will. And Helen, it's really good to see you."

The woman smiled. "I'll be in the kitchen if you need me."

Trish entered the parlor and stopped short. Her breath caught in her throat, her shoulders sagged. Hurtful memories entered her mind and threatened to exhaust the last shred of her energy. She hadn't expected this, to feel such overwhelming sadness. She'd put the divorce on hold for nearly a year, unable to face the failure, but now, being here and stepping into this room again after all this time, brought everything back.

She and Clay had argued—it had become nearly impossible not to during those days—right before she left for an overnight business trip. Trish had come home later that evening when the trip was unexpectedly canceled. With makeup sex on her mind, she strode into the parlor eager to see her husband and put a happy ending on the evening.

She found Clay with Suzy Johnson. On the sofa. Together. Intimately sipping wine and quietly laughing about God only knows, some private joke they'd probably shared. Everything about that scene screamed "wrong" in a marriage already precariously holding on by a thread. And the last thing she'd needed was the hometown girl, a Worth family friend, hovering, waiting in the wings for a chance at Clay.

Trish ground her teeth, reminding herself that she couldn't dwell on that now. She couldn't look back. She took a seat, spreading out the baby's blanket and then laid the baby down. Meggie stared up at her with sparkling eyes, kicking her legs like an exercise guru, happy to be stretching out. That's when Trish saw moisture leaking from the baby's bloomers.

"Oh, darn," she muttered. She'd left the diaper bag in the

taxi. She chewed on her lower lip again and shook her head. She had more-than-average intelligence, but Trish couldn't have predicted in a thousand years how difficult being a single mom would be.

Motherhood was kicking her butt.

"Have patience with me, sweet baby. I'm still learning."

Just then Clay strode into the room with his usual confident swagger, and her heartbeats sped watching him move across the floor. His jaw tight, and his face flawlessly chiseled from granite, Trish had almost forgotten how handsome he was. She'd almost forgotten his raw sensuality. That and his innate charm had turned her head, even though she'd fought it tooth and nail in the beginning of their relationship. Because while she had refused Clayton Worth's romantic advances, she hadn't refused to represent him as his publicist and she'd taken him on as a client. Landing a country superstar even in the final stages of his music career had been a big deal and she'd never mixed business with pleasure. But Clay had other ideas, setting his sights on her. Once she'd stopped resisting the irresistible, she'd fallen deeply in love.

"You're the perfect woman for me," he'd say, before covering her body with his and bringing them both...*perfection*. And she'd actually believed it for a while.

He came to a halt a few feet in front of her, a pink polka-dot diaper bag gripped in his hand. "Is this what you need?"

Her gaze traveled from the tight fit of his blue jeans, to a shining silver belt buckle with the famous W brand, up the wide expanse of his blue chambray shirt to his throat and the hairs that peeked out from underneath the collar. She'd loved to kiss that part of his throat and nibble her way up to his mouth. She lifted her gaze further to meet with russet-brown eyes that seemed to peer into her soul. At one time, he could melt her heart with just one of those penetrating looks. She wondered if he was melting Suzy Johnson's heart now.

"Oh, uh, yes. Thank you."

He set the diaper bag down near the sofa and then sat opposite her on a wing chair. Leaning in, he braced his arms on his knees. With a no-holds-barred expression, he asked, "Are you ready to tell me what's going on?"

She'd procrastinated telling Clay about Meggie partly because she could hardly believe it herself and partly because she knew how much Clay had wanted his own family. To her knowledge, no one had ever really denied Clay anything. He'd hit country music stardom at a young age and had retired in this mid-thirties to run the Worth empire. He was wealthy, good-looking and admired, a man used to having things on his own terms. Trish often thought of him as the golden boy. Everything in his life had come easy, whereas the opposite had been true for her.

She'd worked hard to build her career, putting her whole heart into it. When Clay moved to the ranch, she'd kept her business in Nashville and split her time between the two places. At the time, he seemed to understand the situation. But having a baby then would have meant Trish having to give up her dream.

As a child, her parents had been so intent on saving her brother from the cancer threatening his life that Trish's needs and wants had been neglected. Every moment and every ounce of their energy went into keeping her younger brother alive. Trish had learned early on to fend for herself and to ward off the neglect by becoming self-reliant and independent. She'd clung to the things that made her strong, her schooling for one, and later, her small thriving business. The thought of letting it go and starting a family wasn't easy for her. Not when she'd finally built something all her own. Not when Clay had changed the rules.

She looked at Clay and began, "Do you remember me telling you about Karin, my childhood friend who lived with her husband in Europe?"

Clay nodded, his eyes narrowing in question. "Yeah, I remember you talking about her."

Trish took a deep breath and pulled a disposable diaper out of the bag. She ran her fingers along the plastic edges. "Well, sadly, her husband died about one year ago. Karin was shattered when she returned to Nashville as a widow. We mourned together. It was only a few weeks later that she found out she was going to have a baby."

Trish glanced at Meggie who had turned her body to peer at Clay with curiosity. The baby had good instincts, Trish thought wryly, trying to keep herself from weeping as she recounted the story. "It was really hard for her. She was pregnant and pretty much alone. I was with her when Meggie was born. Oh, Clay, it was such a mir—"

But Trish couldn't finish her thought, not without falling apart. Meggie *was* a miracle—just seeing her being born, all wrinkly and pink, taking her first breaths and crying her first soft cries, had been a life-changing experience for Trish. She'd never expected to feel such incredible awe and wonder.

Clay sat quietly, listening, and Trish continued. "Karin had complications after the delivery that put her life at risk. It was touch and go for months and then last month, she got an infection that she just couldn't fight off."

Trish closed her eyes, willing the grief away as those painful memories surfaced. "She made me promise I'd take the baby if things went bad. I agreed, of course."

She'd promised her friend, but Trish never thought that she'd have to follow through on that promise. She never believed her friend would die. The baby had been thrust into her life and now she was solely responsible for her. "Karin didn't make it and I'm Meggie's legal guardian now," she explained. "I plan to adopt her as soon as I can."

Clay's eyes softened as he peered at Meggie. "The baby has no other family?"

"I'm it, for all practical purposes." Karin's mother was in a nursing home. Her husband's parents were gone.

She fumbled with Meggie's diaper. She never got the thing on straight the first time and she'd learned the hard way what happened when there was a leak. She refastened the diaper, making it fit a little better. "I'm muddling through," she confessed. "This is all so new to me." She looked up to find Clay's eyes on her. "Meggie had a little fever last week and I couldn't travel with her until she was completely healthy."

He waited a beat. "That's why you arrived late?"

Trish nodded. "That's the only reason."

She'd agreed to live in the guesthouse for one month and work on publicity for Penny's Song. And while she was here, they would end things legally, their marriage only a few terms and a divorce signature away from being history.

"Under the circumstances, I'm surprised you showed up at all."

She shook her head. "I wouldn't miss being a part of Penny's Song. I…it's still important to me, Clay. Because of what my brother went through, and even more so now that I have a child." She cringed once the words were out, wondering if his eyes would grow hard and resentment would tighten the sharp angles of his face even more. When neither of those things happened, Trish was hit with reality and unrelenting sadness.

He's divorcing you, Trish. He doesn't care anymore.

She'd been served those divorce papers a few short months after she'd walked out on him, but she hadn't had the heart to end things. Even though she'd tried to forget him, coming face-to-face with Clay now brought it all full circle and her heart ached for the loss. Once upon a time, they'd been so much in love. But everything had changed. She was a single mother and she had to get her life in order. She'd see the end of one dream and the beginning of another.

After she replaced Meggie's bloomers, she picked up the freshly diapered baby and cuddled her close. "All clean now."

Meggie clung to her, laying her head on Trish's shoulder. Blond locks tickled her throat and Trish smiled as she lifted her gaze to Clay. She saw the slightest flicker in his eyes.

He rose from his seat and took a few steps toward her. She caught a whiff of his aftershave, the scent of spice and musk filling her mind with images of moonlit trysts on silken sheets and beds of straw. They'd made love every place imaginable on the ranch.

"You should have told me about her, Trish."

"You should have answered my phone calls."

His mouth twisted and they stared at each other. Both stubborn when they thought they were right, they butted heads often. "Besides, it wasn't as if we're sharing much of our lives anymore."

Clay scrubbed his jaw and sighed deeply. "Let's get you settled in the guesthouse."

With the baby in her arms, Trish got up from her seat and grabbed for the diaper bag. Before she could sling it over her shoulder, Clay intervened, reaching for the bag. "I've got it."

His fingers brushed hers. Inwardly she gasped from the intense heat. Electricity coursed through her system potent enough to curl the very tips of her toes. And when she looked at Clay, his eyes gleamed with something he couldn't conceal. He'd felt the connection, too.

They stood there for half a beat, no one moving, staring into each other's eyes.

A woman's singsong voice coming from the entry broke the moment. "Hello, Clay. Are you in here?" They turned their heads at the same time toward the doorway. The voice grew louder as the woman neared the room. "I made sugar cookies for Penny's Song and thought you'd like some."

Suzy Johnson walked through the doorway, a bright smile on her face, wearing a summery sundress with big yellow and blue flowers. The minute she glided inside and spotted Trish with Clay, she froze. "Oh! S-sorry if I'm interrupting. Helen didn't answer the door and…well, it was open. I didn't know you had—"

"It's okay, Suzy," Clay said. "Thanks for the cookies."

She nodded, but the moment she took notice of the blond-haired, blue-eyed baby in Trish's arms, her cheeks paled in color and she nearly dropped her cookie platter.

Clay's family *friend* had been forever stopping by, bringing over cherry pies, asking Clay for favors or reminiscing about their childhood in Red Ridge. Whenever the hometown girl was around, Trish felt like an outsider, so seeing her discomfort now gave her no small measure of satisfaction.

The baby let out a little cry, interrupting the deafening silence. Trish rocked Meggie gently and met the dark-haired woman's silver-dollar-sized stare.

Another moment ticked by. Trish wouldn't engage in conversation with her, and Clay wasn't uttering a word.

"I'll…I guess I'll leave these with Helen in the kitchen," she stammered, wielding her cookie dish and backing out of the room.

Finally.

Once she was gone, Trish turned to Clay, cutting off anything he might say and managing to keep the pain from her voice. "I see nothing has changed around here."

Two

A tick worked in Clay's jaw as he strode silently beside her. Every so often his gaze would shift to the baby Trish held in her arms, otherwise he kept his focus toward the guesthouse that lay fifty yards away from the main house. Trish was too tired to deal with his sour mood right now.

Granted, she hadn't been his wife in the real sense in over a year, but you'd think he'd inform Suzy Johnson to stay the hell away until the ink on the final divorce decree was dry. But that was Suzy, always cheery, always showing up uninvited and always bearing treats.

Trish bristled. The sooner she signed those divorce papers the better.

She turned her thoughts to more pressing matters. Getting Meggie settled and comfortable was her first priority. Trish was an avid planner. She banked her livelihood on her organizational skills. She made lists. She set goals. She could plot out her future months in advance. It was the main reason she'd been successful as a publicist. She had a knack for scoping out musicians' careers long-range and took great pleasure in seeing them come to fruition.

But she had no plan for motherhood. None. She was learning the hard way that babies didn't *do* schedules. They couldn't be predicted. Their needs were ever-changing and she would be the one adapting, not the other way around.

Every day brought a new challenge. Every day was different, unplanned and unorganized. It was a whole new learning curve for her.

When they reached the entrance, Clay unlocked the door and allowed her entry first. He stepped inside behind her. "Your luggage is in the master bedroom."

She turned to him. "Thank you."

He nodded and moved into the living area, tossing the diaper bag down on the light tan leather sofa.

Trish followed him into the room. Once upon a time, Trish had fallen in love with the small cottage and had asked Clay if she could make a few changes, put her stamp on it, so to speak. She gazed into the room with a sense of pride. A combination of soft leather and suede in cream tones marked the Southwest contemporary feel of the house. Delicate copper and brass sculptures sat on glass tables and masterful metal artwork hung on the walls. She'd created a cozy atmosphere in keeping with the flavor of Red Ridge for their one-time guests.

But it looked as if no one had ever stepped foot in it. Everything was in its place, not a stick of furniture or a fruit bowl had been moved. The place was perfect and pristine. That would change in the blink of an eye.

Babies caused chaos, even four-month-olds who weren't at the crawling stage yet. Meggie did her fair share of rolling, though, and Trish knew she had to give the baby a wide berth when she set her down on the floor.

"If the baby needs anything, Helen will be around. She's got three grandchildren."

"*Three* now? She had only two when I was living, uh, here," she finished awkwardly.

Clay waited a beat, probably deciding whether to enter into a conversation with her. The tick in his jaw did an intermittent dance. "Jillie had another, a boy this time."

"So Helen has two grandsons and a granddaughter. I bet they keep her busy."

"When she's not here, she's usually with them."

Trish often wondered if her own mother would take to Meggie like that, love her unconditionally and accept her in their family. It seemed Trish's mother had given everything she had to give to Blake in those earlier years. Once he'd recovered, her mother had never really been the same. Maybe it was the pressure, the constant tension or the drain his illness had taken on her, but her mother hadn't really been thrilled at the prospect of a grandchild. Not the way Trish had hoped.

The baby squirmed in her arms, wiggling and making her presence known. Clay watched her interact with the baby with curious eyes. "I'd better set her down for a few seconds."

She bent to put Meggie down on her butt, propping her against the sofa on the floor. The baby waved her arms and cackled, happy for the time being. "There you go, sweet baby. Much better, huh?" Straightening, she turned to Clay. "She likes a change of scenery sometimes. I've got to learn not to hold her all the time."

His gaze stayed on Meggie sitting quite contentedly on the floor. "You need help unpacking?"

He was being polite. Clay had always been a gentleman, even when he was hopping mad. She shook her head. "No. We'll be fine, Clay."

His mouth pinched tight and he lifted his eyes to her. "Doesn't the baby need a crib?"

At least Trish had that much under control. "I'll call the rental company and have a few things delivered tomorrow."

"What about tonight? Where will she sleep?"

Trish let out a pent-up breath. "She'll be with me. The truth is, I don't get much sleep. I check on her most of the night. She sleeps so soundly, sometimes I wonder if she's breathing at all. I guess most new moms go through the same kind of panic."

Clay nodded as if he understood it all, but she noted the question in his eyes. No one knew what parenthood was like until they experienced it themselves. Trish's emotions this past month were all over the map, from highs when Meggie would take a full bottle and fall asleep, to lows when she was fussy and Trish couldn't figure out what the heck was wrong. Half the time, she second-guessed herself and questioned if she was doing *anything* right. But Meggie was thriving and safe, so she clung to those positive thoughts.

"Helen stocked the refrigerator. You should have everything you need in there," Clay said.

"Okay. And I'd like to see Penny's Song as soon as possible."

The divorce wasn't the only reason she'd come back to Red Ridge. She'd promised to play a key role in fundraising for Penny's Song, even though that hadn't been the original plan. *That plan,* to be there for its development and construction, had gone by the wayside when her marriage fell apart.

"Tomorrow morning soon enough?"

"Yes, I can hardly wait. I've been thinking about it. Wondering. Is it…all that we imagined?"

Clay's unyielding expression softened. "It's all that and more. Seeing the kids there, well, it makes all the difference."

Young Penny Martin, the charity's namesake, a Red Ridge local and a big fan of Clayton Worth, hadn't been as lucky as Trish's brother, Blake. Even though she'd put up a valiant fight and had been so brave, she'd lost her life to leukemia at the age of ten. Her death sparked the idea in Clay to use Worth land and resources for the charity and Trish had been behind it one-hundred percent. Penny's Song would go a long way in helping kids robbed of their childhood assimilate back into society after their recovery by making them feel normal again. Trish couldn't wait to see how the facility had come to life.

"We'll be ready."

"I can drive you over at nine, if that's not too early?"

"Early? I wish. Meggie's up at the crack of dawn. By 9:00 a.m. I've already put in half a day."

Clay wasn't really paying attention to her, though. She caught him watching Meggie, who had plunked down onto her tummy and begun to roll toward the fireplace. "Looks like you've got a runaway."

"Meggie!" By the time the words were out of her mouth, Clay was there, picking her up before she pulled the fireplace tools on top of her.

"You're fast," he said. The smile on his face was only for Meggie. He held her at a distance for a second, not quite sure what to do with her. Then he tucked her into his body and cradled her to his chest.

Trish inhaled a sharp breath.

Meggie wasn't too sure what to make of Clay, but she wasn't crying either. Trish wished she could say the same of herself. Inside, her heart cried out seeing what could have been if only their marriage had survived. Clayton Worth, the big, rugged cowboy holding a baby, *her baby,* in his strong arms was a tender sight to behold.

She could have gone on watching the two of them, but Clay didn't give her time to lament the loss. Before she knew it, he was handing Meggie over. "Here you go." He made the transfer with utmost care. "She's going to keep you on your toes."

"She's fast," Trish whispered, still awed seeing Clay holding the baby. "But she's a good sleeper, so it's a trade-off."

Clay nodded, giving Meggie one long look before turning on his heels and heading to the door. With his hand on the doorknob, he glanced back Trish's way. "If you change your mind, I can send Helen over to help you unpack."

"I'll be fine."

Clay sent her a dubious look before walking out.

Trish closed her eyes. Heaven help her. The last half hour had been one of the hardest in her life. Seeing Clay again *hurt*. The pain had resurfaced the minute he'd walked up to greet her. And seeing him holding Meggie just now was like pouring salt in her freshly opened wound.

He couldn't wait to send you divorce papers.

He never really understood you.

He's probably having a hot and heavy affair with Suzy.

They were all good reasons to keep Clay at a distance and not get suckered in by his deadly good looks, heart-melting smile or sentimental memories of the good times they'd shared.

He was *then*. This was *now*.

She may not have a handle on motherhood yet, but she knew everything about surviving and remembering why she'd come back to the ranch was a priority.

Divorce.

Clay's boots ate concrete as he strode toward his house. Trish had a kid. *A baby.* He wondered how long it would take for him to wrap his mind around that. She'd blown their marriage apart denying him a child. He never understood why she'd been so resistant to the idea. He had money and resources to provide for a child better than ninety-nine-point-nine percent of the population of the world. She hadn't trusted in that. She hadn't trusted in him enough to know they'd work it out. And then she'd started in with her accusations about him and Suzy.

Trish's appearance today tilted him off balance. His head spun seeing her again, and he swore up and down about the decision to bring her here. His attorney could have dealt with the divorce and to hell with Trish's fundraising abilities. He would've found someone else for the job. But he was thick-headed and wanted things done his way. He wanted to face her again, after she'd walked out. He wanted closure and to end things civilly. That had been the plan.

It was still the plan, he reminded himself.

He entered the house, his stomach clenched tight, and shut the door with too much force. Behind him the beveled glass rattled from the slam.

"That you, Clayton?" He heard Helen's muffled voice from a distance.

There was a bang. Then another. Lifting his head to listen closely, he strode toward the stairs. "Helen?"

Boom. Thump.

"Up here."

He strode toward the staircase and the clatter that interrupted the peace in the house. "Where are you?"

"In the attic. I need help."

"I'm coming. Hold on." Clay jogged up the stairs quickly, taking them two at a time. He reached the landing and turned the corner quickly, finding a pull-down ladder that led to another small landing and the attic door.

He yanked it open just as Helen popped her head out and they nearly bumped. He examined her face, dotted with grime, but the rest of her appeared uninjured. "What the hell—"

"We've got baby equipment up here, Clayton. Took some

shoving and pushing, but I found your old crib. There are sheets that need some gentle washing, but everything is in excellent condition."

Clay sighed with relief. He glanced at the boxes, crates and furniture Helen had obviously moved. "You shouldn't have come up here by yourself. You could have gotten hurt."

She waved him off as she was prone to do. "Nonsense. We need to get this stuff down for that little baby to use."

"Trish is taking care of that. She's renting equipment. It should arrive tomorrow."

"That woman needs all the help she can get with that baby."

Clay didn't take offense. Helen never meddled in his love life, so there was no ulterior motive in her comment. He knew exactly what she meant. Trish looked frazzled when she arrived and she was probably exhausted by now, chasing the human rolling pin around.

There'd be no arguing with Helen anyway. She was like a mother to him, even if they'd never spoken of such things. She'd been around Clay and his brothers Tagg and Jackson since they were youngsters.

"Fine," he said. "I'll bring it over."

Two hours later, Clay had the crib set up in the master bedroom in the guesthouse.

Meggie was sleeping on a thick quilt with a zoo animal motif on the living room floor. When he'd knocked, Trish had been surprised to see him again, but there was a grateful look in her eyes and Clay knew he'd done the right thing bringing the crib over. The baby was innocent in all this and she shouldn't have to do without creature comforts.

Clay gave the sides of the crib a few tugs, checking that he had the screws tight and secure before he backed away to admire his work. The crib was made of solid walnut and was in fantastic shape for as old as it was. When he turned, he found Trish in the room holding a glass of iced tea with three slices of lemon submerged under the ice.

"Here you go," she said, offering him the glass.

He took a gulp and swallowed the cool liquid. "Just the way I like it."

"Some things never change," she said with a shrug.

Was that another crack or just a casual comment?

"I can't thank you enough," she said, lifting the crib sheets from the dresser and moving to the crib. Judging by her sincere tone, he gave her the benefit of the doubt. She'd remembered the way he took his tea, nothing more. "You didn't have to do this tonight, but I'm sure Meggie will love her new digs."

Clay didn't want to smile, yet the corner of his mouth quirked up. He wanted out of there, away from Trish. She'd showered and changed into a pair of jeans and a red plaid blouse, but even the simple clothes looked fashionable and elegant on her. Her blond hair was still damp and curling around her face and shoulders. She smelled of citrus and sugar like a sweet piece of fruit.

"I'd better go."

Trish nodded, holding the freshly cleaned sheets to her chest. "I'll walk you out."

She followed behind as he walked into the living room. The baby took that moment to wake up and look at him from the quilt. She made a little sound, watching him cut across the room with eyes wide and bluer than a spring lake. She was a cute little thing, all pink cheeks and tiny blond curls.

"Well, look who's awake now," Trish offered in a sugary voice. When he glanced at her, her attention was focused on the baby.

He reached for the doorknob. He didn't belong here. He wasn't part of this happy scenario.

"Good night," he said as Trish bent to pick Meggie up. The two of them clung to each other.

Mother and child.

"Good night, Clay."

He opened the door and closed it behind him without looking back.

He'd done his good deed for the day.

Getting the baby up in the morning, fed, bathed and dressed was a whirlwind of activity and a ritual that hadn't gotten any easier for Trish. By the time nine o'clock rolled around, Trish was putting the finishing touches on her own grooming. She brushed her teeth quickly, secured her hair in a ponytail, then mascara tipped her eyelashes and slashed light pink lipstick on her lips.

She was excited and eager to see Penny's Song for the first time. She'd only seen the place laid out on drafting paper, the design one she'd worked on with Clay. She wondered if the real thing would meet her expectations.

When the doorbell rang, Trish was as ready as she'd ever be. She had a diaper bag filled with essentials, a well-fed, well-rested baby and nerves of steel. At least that's what she told herself.

She went to the door braced to see Clay again. Today she'd make an appointment with him to discuss the divorce. No sense putting off the inevitable. Suzy Johnson would then have a legal right to get her claws into him.

When she opened the door, surprise registered when it wasn't Clay but a pretty brunette standing on the doorstep.

"Hi, I'm Callie Worth. Tagg's wife. I hope it's okay that I stopped by?"

"Hi, Callie. Of course it is." Trish still had friends in Red Ridge. She'd heard that Tagg had gotten married. Callie and she were, for all intents and purposes, sisters-in-law at the moment. "I'm Trish. It's nice to meet you. Would you like to come in?"

"I'm dying to come in, but I know you're going over to Penny's Song in a little while."

When Trish raised her brows, she explained. "I spoke to Clay this morning and he told me your plans and that…that you had a baby."

"He told you about Meggie?"

"He said she was a pretty little picture."

Trish smiled. "Well, I sure think so."

"We're expecting a baby soon, too."

Trish glanced at the little pooch of a belly jutting out from under Callie's blouse. "Congratulations. I'm happy for you and Tagg. There's, uh, nothing like it." That much was true. Even though she was still sorting it all out, she wouldn't trade having Meggie for the world.

The baby's cry from the other room startled her. "Oh, I'd better get her. Come in, please."

Callie followed her into the master bedroom and they found Meggie in her crib, rolling from her back to her belly. She stopped and looked up when she noted a new face.

"This is Meggie," Trish said.

The baby was dressed in springtime yellow bib overalls with a giant purple daisy on the front and matching bootie socks.

"Hello, Meggie," Callie said. "You look ready for a stroll in the Easter parade." She turned from the baby to Trish with sympathy in her eyes. "I heard about what happened to your friend. I'm sorry."

"Karin was a good friend. I…miss her."

"You're being the best friend a girl could have. Making sure her daughter is loved and nurtured. I, well, I think it's pretty wonderful of you."

"Thank you." Uncomfortable with the praise, she changed the subject. "Do you know what you're having?"

Callie laid a hand on her stomach and shook her head. "Not yet. It's a little too soon to tell. Secretly, I think Tagg wants a boy, but he's really not saying."

When she didn't say the cliché, *as long as it's healthy,* which was a given for any soon-to-be parents, Trish decided she really liked Callie.

"When I spoke with Clay he said you were renting baby gear and, well, I'm hoping I can help. Tagg went a little crazy the other day when we went shopping. We have two of almost everything."

"Honestly?"

Callie smiled and a look of love entered her eyes. It was sweet enough to envy, just a little. "I'm not joking. Tagg was like a kid in a candy store. Big mistake on my part taking him to look at baby furniture, but now his extravagance might come in handy. If you need a stroller, play yard or high chair, you're looking at Baby Central. We can loan you anything you need. We won't need it for months."

Normally, Trish wouldn't accept such an offer, but Callie was sincere and kind about it, looking like she really wanted to help. Trish wouldn't refuse her good intentions. Not to mention that the loan would save her time and money. "Oh my gosh, that would be incredible."

Callie's face brightened. "Great. I'll bring the stroller over to Penny's Song and Meggie can test it out today."

"That's so…I don't know what to say. Thank you."

"You're welcome. I'd better run, Clay will be—"

"Clay will be what?"

They turned to find Clay leaning against the doorframe, a curious expression on his face. With boots crossed, a black shirt tucked into worn jeans and hair peeking out from a tan suede Stetson, he didn't just look the part. There was no doubt he was a rancher through and through—a tall, lean, rugged cowboy with a destructive smile and melt-your-heart eyes.

"Here. And now you are." Callie walked over to her brother-in-law and gave him a quick hug. "See you later at the little ranch. Bye, Trish."

"Bye, Callie."

Meeting Tagg's wife had lifted her mood. She hadn't expected such a warm, friendly welcome. "She's nice," Trish said, once Callie was gone.

"Yeah," Clay answered, losing the smile he'd reserved for Callie. "Listen, before we go anywhere, I want to talk to you."

"About the divorce? Yes, I want to set up a time to discuss it, too."

Clay shook his head and walked farther into the room. "Fine, we'll do that. But first, I want to discuss something else."

He sounded serious. Trish glanced at Meggie who was occupying herself for the moment. They had a few minutes, at best. "Okay."

Clay gestured to the bed as he walked farther into the room. She sat on the edge closest to the crib and he sat on the opposite corner. He took his hat off and set it down between them. "It's about Suzy."

Trish's good mood vanished. Her stomach knotted at the mention of her name. Images popped into her mind of all the times Suzy had come over, right after she'd divorced her alcoholic husband. At first, Trish had felt sorry for her and offered friendship, but within a matter of weeks, it had become clear that Suzy had only wanted Clay's friendship. Tagg and Jackson liked her. Wes liked her. Everyone was always singing her praises, so Trish tolerated her, but that tolerance had worn thin until one day it finally snapped.

"Whatever's happening with you and Suzy is no longer any of my business."

It was a big fat lie, but she clung to it and sent him a smile that could melt butter.

A noisy breath whooshed out of him and the irritated sound filled the room. His dark eyes went cold. "Your assumptions could fill a football stadium."

"Oh, I know. Suzy's a friend. Your family has known her family for—"

"Cut it out, Trish." Clay kept his voice low, mindful of the baby in the room, but she couldn't miss the warning in his voice. "It's not what you think. It never was."

The soft sounds of a rattle, like sifting sand, turned their attention toward the crib. Meggie cooed and Trish focused on the contented baby while she got a grip on her feelings. She turned to him. "It doesn't matter anymore."

"Look," Clay said firmly. "I wanted you to know you're gonna see Suzy around the ranch. She's volunteering her free time at Penny's Song. We value her nursing skills and I'm not going to waste my breath defending myself whenever you *think* you see something going on between us."

"You weren't defending yourself yesterday when she popped over with cookies."

"That's right, *cookies*. Besides, would it have done any good? Your mind was pretty much set."

"That woman has perfect timing," Trish muttered, "showing up just when I arrived." She rose, keeping her composure, and moved toward the crib to check on Meggie. The baby complained with a little cry and Trish stroked her head gently, then put the rattle back in her hand. Satisfied, Meggie gripped the toy and began shaking it again.

"It wasn't planned. Truth is, I haven't seen much of Suzy outside of Penny's Song."

Trish didn't believe that. How could she? The woman had

walked into Clay's home yesterday like she owned the place. Like she belonged there, and Trish didn't.

"The last time I saw you two together…" Trish struggled with the memory that had been the final blow to her marriage. "She showed up at our home when she knew darn well I would be out of town for the night."

"She didn't just show up. I invited her."

Stunned, Trish blinked. What kind of lame admission was that? It was a low blow and her heart ached, *again*. She couldn't forget how it felt that night walking into her home, hoping to mend her marriage only to find the two of them going behind her back, sitting on the sofa, all cozy-like, whispering and joking around, with wineglasses half-emptied. She'd felt like an outsider in her own home. She'd felt betrayed in the worst possible way. Suzy had usurped her position, looking smug when Trish found them together. It had been the last straw. Trish had raced upstairs and began packing her bags.

Their marriage had gotten difficult and Clay couldn't handle it. Trish shouldn't have been surprised because he'd done the same in his relationships with women who'd come before her and yet the injury stuck like a knife to her heart. She'd been foolish enough to think that what they'd had was different, *real*.

"And there you have it," she finally said, boiling with anger.

Clay rose to his feet. His eyes narrowed and the muscle in his jaw pounded against his cheek. With slow calculated steps, he came toward her, his voice deep and uncompromising. "I don't like being falsely accused. I'm clearing the air now, once and for all. Nothing happened that night."

"You've never slept with her?" She barked her question.

"No." He answered immediately with fierceness in his eyes that made Trish rethink her certainty.

"Have you kissed her?"

He stared at her, sucked in a breath and then looked away.

"You have!" There was no way to hide her accusation.

He snapped his attention back to her. "Damn it, Trish. You ran off and left me."

"No one's ever done that to you before." His ego couldn't take the blow. Or maybe he'd realized he didn't love her anymore. Whatever the reason, Clay hadn't tried to mend their marriage. He'd just accepted her decision and let her go.

"No, not really, but that's not the point. You ran."

"And you didn't do a damn thing about it."

Old feelings of rejection and abandonment had nearly destroyed her. All she'd wanted from him was some sort of halfway valiant effort to get her back. He'd made two phone calls. *Two,* that hadn't gotten them anywhere. The sum total of their marriage hadn't amounted to much. "You couldn't wait to file for divorce."

"You played a part in our breakup, in case you're forgetting." He sighed. "Either you believe me or you don't about Suzy. But I wanted a fresh slate before we started working together."

Trish couldn't let it go. Not now. Not with this new information that Clay had never admitted to before. "Why did you invite Suzy over that night?"

Clay scrubbed his jaw, his way of stalling for time. "I needed her opinion about something."

"That's all?" She would've laughed if it wasn't so darn serious. "That's what you're giving me?"

A wry smile lifted the corner of his mouth. "It's something I wanted to *give* you—having to do with the Worth family heirloom."

"The ruby necklace?" Astonished, Trish's eyes widened. She'd heard tales about the necklace that had been in the family for generations. The ranch had been in the throes of ruination and would have crumbled if not for Chance Worth, Clay's great-great-great-grandfather. Legend had it the necklace played a vital role in the ranch's salvation and had brought Lizzie and Chance Worth together over one hundred years ago. Trish had never laid eyes on it. Clay had it locked away in a bank vault for safekeeping.

But none of this made any sense. She and Clay hadn't been getting along. The last thing he'd do would be to gift a precious piece of family jewelry to a wife he wasn't sure he wanted, a wife who refused to just have children whenever he snapped his fingers.

"Not the necklace, but a ring I was having made for you that would have matched."

"Oh." The confusion rushing through her was powerful and tipped her well-placed conviction on end. "Why didn't you tell me this before?"

Clay leveled a gaze at her, making sure she understood. "I was royally pissed. Your accusations burned me. You should have known I wouldn't—"

"How? How would I know that?" Trish wouldn't back down.

"With you, it was different. I never wanted to marry any of those other women I dated. I married you and I thought you knew what that meant. Trust is trust. Either you have it or you don't."

He made it seem so easy, so uncomplicated, yet Trish knew it wasn't. Having complete faith was something Trish had never been able to master in life. She'd been disappointed too many times to count. Hope did not spring eternal with her. "It's not always that simple, Clay."

He squared his shoulders, his voice low, filled with recrimination. "Sometimes it is, Trish."

Meggie fussed in her crib and began to squirm around. Her baby's patience was at its limit. She wanted out. Trish went to her. She needed the time to think, to let Clay's revelation sink in. Not that it mattered anymore. She wasn't sure she could believe him. And what did *that* say about their marriage?

She lifted Meggie out of the crib and nestled her to her chest. Meggie settled down, yet Trish had been the one comforted. Just by holding her. Drinking in her sweetness and listening to her little cooing sounds. The chaotic peace the baby lent her was unqualified. "I think we should go."

Clay looked fit to be tied and unwilling to concede the point. "Let's get out of here."

Three

It was nothing short of a miracle.

Clay stopped his truck on a low rise that overlooked Penny's Song. Trish squinted against the morning glare as they got out of the truck and focused on the little ranch below. A hum of accomplishment and intense pride prickled her senses. She felt the humming clear down to her toes as she leaned on the hood of the car. This had been their dream, together. It wasn't a facade from an old Western movie set, but the real deal. Their vision had come alive right before her eyes. "Oh, Clay."

"I know," he said quietly. Nothing had been resolved between them, not that she expected it, but at least they had this. And it was something. She would have been by his side to see Penny's Song come to fruition if she'd still been living here. If their marriage hadn't fallen apart. But that wasn't what mattered the most to her.

What mattered were the children who would benefit from

Penny's Song. In a small way or maybe even in larger ways, their lives would be forever changed by coming here. They'd have chores and jobs to do. They'd make friends from different parts of the country. They'd feel worthy of good health, working and building their bodies in ways that were natural and God-given.

She thought of her brother and how hard it had been for him after his recovery. When he went back to school, he'd been a fish out of water. He felt out of touch, unable to relate to his friends any longer. His normalcy wasn't theirs and it had showed. A place like Penny's Song would have helped him. He would have been with other children who were experiencing the same adjustment in their lives.

"It's a work in progress," Clay stated, his voice a deep rasp. "This being the first week and all."

From this distance, the children looked like miniatures. She saw a few of them near the barn, a few by the corrals, and one little girl chasing a chicken. The buildings were colorful and brightly decorated, yet with an air of authenticity. She made out the general store and the saloon, a place designated for mealtimes. Kids would help set up the dining area, eat there and have KP duty afterward. The bunkhouse was a building set a ways apart, where the children and the counselors, otherwise known as the ranch foremen, would spend their evenings.

"How many are here this week?"

"Eight, so far. Ranging from seven to fourteen years old. Next week, we'll have a dozen kids."

Absently, she laid a hand on his forearm, overcome with emotion. Tears welled in her eyes and she fought them valiantly, but she couldn't shake the notion that the creation of Penny's Song had been the baby that she and Clay never had, the one thing that they'd both loved from conception. "It's amazing, Clay."

His gaze slid to the hand that touched him. She'd over-stepped a boundary and was ready to pull her hand away. But he placed his palm over hers and held it there. "Yeah, I can't deny it's a good thing."

"Yes," she whispered, closing her eyes for a second. Comfort seeped in and her heart swelled. There was an overriding sense of peace that crossed between them, much like two parents watching their child take their first steps. They stood together on the hill, looking out at the charitable dude ranch they'd conceived together. For the moment, it felt right.

Meggie grumbled from the car seat, breaking the sacred moment, and Trish left Clay to check on her. He'd put the car seat in the back end of the Silverado's cab and the baby, facing backward for safety's sake, was fidgeting now, eager to get a move on.

He popped his head in from the front window. "She okay?"

"She's fine," she answered. "Just wants to be in on the action."

"We should get moving then." Clay bounded inside the truck and started the engine.

Trish took her seat and the baby quieted now that the truck was on the road. When they reached the entrance to Penny's Song, Clay parked and cut the engine.

They began the tour at the general store with Clay holding the diaper bag and Meggie in Trish's arms. The baby was intrigued with the bright colors and the ranch animals, but mostly by the children who had seen the purple-and-yellow flower child and wanted to meet her.

"This is Meggie," Trish said to one little girl who'd run up to them just as they were exiting the general store. She bent to the girl's level, noting her big expressive eyes and the new growth of golden curls covering her scalp. "She'll be five months old soon."

The girl smiled. "She's cute."

"What's your name?" Trish asked.

"Wendy."

"It's nice to meet you, Wendy."

Meggie reached out to touch Wendy's freckled cheek. The girl chuckled and announced, "I'm going on eight. I live in Flagstaff. Is she sick?"

There was curious concern on the girl's face. Trish glanced at Clay. His expression faltered. Although he made an effort to hide it, she saw the way his eyes narrowed and his body jerked a fraction of an inch. She wasn't going down alone. Clay was just as affected as she was.

"Oh, no. She's not. She's…healthy."

Wendy ripped Trish's barriers to shreds and opened the wound that she'd lived with since Blake took sick. Children shouldn't have to deal with illness. They should be free to enjoy their childhood without pain touching their lives. She shared a bittersweet moment with Clay, a wink in time, before returning her attention to the child.

A boy named Eddie walked up to see Meggie next and Trish made introductions all over again. Soon all eight of the children had left their chores behind to meet the baby. They were curious and the questions came fast and furiously. Trish didn't mind answering them. She'd kept it simple. Yes, Meggie was her baby. No, Meggie didn't have any brothers or sisters. Yes, she was from out of town. No, the baby couldn't talk yet.

Her daughter kicked enthusiastically, responding to the children and the attention she received.

One by one, the children resumed their chores and Trish found herself alone with Clay again. "The saloon is really the mess hall," he said as they headed there. "We've got the kids on mess duty. They don't work, they don't eat."

"You old meany."

"They like the idea. At least up until yesterday, they liked the idea."

Trish smiled. "It'll get old fast."

"Maybe," Clay said. "But life'll come at them whether they are ready for it or not. It's all a learning process."

Wise words, Trish thought.

They were entering the saloon when Callie strode up behind them with a light charcoal baby stroller. Unisex coloring, Trish mused, with big rubber wheels that wouldn't falter on the ranch's rugged terrain.

"Well, what do you think of Meggie's new ride?" Callie asked. "Tagg had to have all the bells and whistles."

"Sounds just like my brother," Clay teased. "He bought the four-wheel drive of strollers."

Callie defended her husband. "You'd do the same, Clayton Worth. You know it."

Clay acquiesced and nodded. "Just waiting for the chance."

Trish froze at the reminder of how badly Clay wanted a family. He was older than her by six years, had had a successful career early in life and was oh-so-ready for children of his own. Trish was just beginning to feel secure in her own career and motherhood was the last thing on her mind. Their timing had been all wrong.

Callie turned her way and realizing the awkward situation, immediately changed the subject. "Let's take Meggie for a test drive."

"Gosh, Callie. Are you sure? It's brand-new and—"

"I'm sure," Callie said graciously. "Looks like I'm just in time, too. The little one looks sleepy."

On the walk over to the saloon, Meggie had slumped heavily in her arms. She probably had jet lag. The commotion from the past few days had tired her out. "She is. She feels like lead weight in my arms right now."

Callie worked at the latches on the stroller. "I'll lower the seat down so the baby can nap."

With that accomplished, Trish laid the baby on the pretty quilted material and strapped her in. Meggie seemed to enjoy her new cushy surroundings and Trish covered her with a lightweight knit blanket she'd pulled from the diaper bag.

"I can stroll her, if you'd like," Callie offered. "It'll give you time to see all of Penny's Song uninterrupted."

Trish inhaled a sharp breath. Her smile wavered. She hadn't seen this coming. She and Meggie had been inseparable for the entire month. How could she let her go? Since Meggie had come into her life, she'd never had a babysitter. No one else had watched her besides Trish. The responsibility weighed on her.

She'll never know neglect. Not ever.

Trish took her role as mother seriously, but she knew she was being overly cautious, if not ridiculous, with Callie.

"Of…of course. You can take her for a stroll."

Callie looked hesitant now and Trish cringed from making her feel awkward in her offer. She finally got her emotions under control and smiled graciously. "It's a great idea."

Callie smiled with relief. "I promise I won't go far."

"Have fun." Trish kept smiling, but her hand covered her heart watching them go.

Clay sidled up next to her. "She'll be fine with Callie."

Mortified she was so obvious, she turned to Clay and sighed. "I know that…*in my head*."

Clay's lips quirked up at the corners and he touched her elbow gently, giving it a tug. "You want to see the rest of this place?"

"Yes, yes, I do." Distracted by his slight touch, she followed him as he led her on the rest of the tour.

Later that afternoon, Clay pulled the truck to a stop in front of the guesthouse. With one hand on the wheel and the other lazy on the console between them, he turned to her. "You made it through the day."

She leaned against the headrest, feeling as tired as the sleeping baby in the car seat behind her. "It turned out even better than we'd expected, didn't it?"

He drew in a breath. "Yeah."

They'd toured the grounds and Trish had gotten a pretty good idea of how the operation worked. She'd been introduced to volunteer counselors who'd assumed roles as foremen on the ranch, the general store "clerk" and the cook, who was responsible for getting the meals prepared each day. Trish visited the stables where she met the string of mellow horses donated to the cause. She'd climbed on the corral fence, watching as Clay's younger brother, Tagg, showed the children the basics of riding and Clay took her to see the tack room and stables the kids were expected to keep clean and tidy. Every child had a list of chores to get through with fun activities sprinkled in during the day.

Tonight they'd have a campfire and sing songs. Tomorrow a chili contest and a hay ride. Every minute of the day meant interaction with the other children and the adult volunteers. Many of the adults were local college students gaining community service experience or simply devoting their time to the charity of their choice.

Trish had a job to do here. It was her contribution to the cause and now she had the picture to go along with the words. She'd be a part of Penny's Song for a short time and being here would help her plan a fundraising event to end all fundraising events.

"It's already a well-oiled machine," Trish said wistfully, enjoying the peace in the cab of the truck. With the baby sleeping, she took time to linger before going inside for round two with Meggie.

"We've got some kinks to work out, but yeah, it's going pretty darn well." Clay spoke with a twinkle in his eyes. Deliberately, she shifted her focus away, gazing out the windshield to the vast Worth pastures. Looking too deeply at her husband could be deadly to her sanity. When he was in a sentimental mood like this with no distractions, nothing to spoil the immediate moment—with just the two of them sitting calmly after a long day—Clayton Worth's charm and appeal knew no rival. "The kinks will shake loose with time."

Clay didn't disagree. "What about your kinks. They loosening up?"

Trish snapped her eyes to his and unwilling to spoil the relaxed mood, she asked simply, "What kinks?"

"You had a hard time with Callie taking Meggie for a walk."

There was no accusation in his tone, and Trish couldn't deny his claim. The entire time Trish walked the perimeter with Clay, she was looking over her shoulder, hoping to get a glimpse of Meggie and make sure she was all right. She'd only half listened to Clay's explanations and commentaries as they toured the facility and she had hoped she wasn't too obvious. "We haven't been separated much," she admitted in earnest.

"She did fine," Clay pointed out.

"But I was a wreck? Is that what you're saying?"

"I wouldn't say *wreck* exactly."

She would have taken offense, but Clay shot her a killer smile, the kind that would normally have buckled her knees. Good thing she was sitting. Now, she could pretend the smile didn't devastate her. "*Concerned* is a better description."

She glanced at Meggie again, catching a glimpse of her at an angle in the rear-facing car seat. The baby had her head slumped against one shoulder, her rosy cheeks even more ruddy now and the tiny curls atop her head catching the fading glow of sunlight.

"I shouldn't keep you," she said softly.

"Will she wake up if we tried to get out?"

"No telling," Trish said honestly. "Meggie always surprises me."

"I'm fine here for a while."

"Babies have the ability to ignore stimuli. They can sleep with environmental sounds and tune them out. She might not wake up. I really should get her inside."

"You've been doing your homework." Again, Clay made the statement without tossing blame her way. He could have been a real hard-ass about her showing up here with a baby in tow and made life difficult for her. But so far, the Worth clan, Helen included, had been understanding, at least about the baby.

"One minute, I'm working on a client's ad campaign for sexy underwear and the next, I'm a brand-new mom, with months of catching up to do. I had to learn fast and I'm barely getting a passing grade."

Clay sucked oxygen into his lungs. "The irony is…"

"Don't say it, Clay." Bringing up the past wouldn't do them any good. She was ready to move on with her life. Meggie was her first priority and that meant shedding the old, even if the old was a drop-dead gorgeous hunk of a man who could turn her inside out without breaking a sweat. Trish hated that they'd come to this.

Clay's cell phone rang and he quickly answered it, mindful of the sleeping baby. Trish heard the sound of a woman's voice on the other end as he carried on a brief, discreet conversation, ending with, "Okay, thanks. I'll stop by later."

She didn't ask about the phone call and he didn't offer to explain, but she'd bet her favorite pair of Justin cowgirl boots that Suzy Johnson would be getting a visit from Clay tonight.

When they got out of the car, Clay took the stroller out of the back end of the truck and Trish unfastened Meggie carefully from the car seat straps. She lifted her and Clay walked beside them in silence as they approached the front door, him pushing an empty stroller.

She let herself in and he followed. He set the stroller inside the entrance and Trish moved to the master bedroom to lay the baby in her crib.

"I'll get the rest of the equipment out of the truck," he said.

Before they'd left Penny's Song, Callie had given her a play yard and a high chair to use as well. The items were still in their boxes. "Want some help?"

Clay shook his head. "I've got it."

When he returned lugging an oblong cardboard box she showed him where she wanted the play yard to go. He followed her into the other bedroom. "This is going to help a lot. While I'm working, Meggie will have a place to play."

"I thought you took time off?" he asked, examining the box, standing it on end.

"There's always some minor crisis or other to deal with. Jodi is good at screening out the potential disasters." Her part-time assistant kept her sane most of the time. The woman was in her mid-forties and had been a single mom, having raised a son on her own. Jodi had had a hard life and never married again. She lived for visits from her now-grown son and since Meggie had come into her life, Trish wondered if she would wind up like Jodi one day.

"Jodi, huh? That woman never liked me."

"What are you talking about? You charmed her socks off from day one."

"You overestimate my appeal." But he chuckled anyway

and then brought the other box containing the high chair inside the house. He set it in the kitchen. "You need help putting this stuff together?"

"Oh, um," Trish stammered, giving it consideration until images flashed of Clay's phone conversation with Suzy. He'd admitted to kissing Suzy and heaven knows what else and the goodwill she'd felt for him shrunk in size. She'd always taken care of herself, no sense in thinking she had Clay to rely on for anything. "No, thank you. I'll deal with it later." There was also no sense in prolonging the inevitable. "I was thinking…we should probably discuss the divorce soon."

Clay's head shot up. He straightened and stared at her. Then he nodded curtly, as if just remembering the reason she'd come to the ranch. The warmth in his eyes faded. "Tomorrow soon enough?"

"Yes, th-that's fine."

"I'll be over at four."

With that, he left her, closing the door behind him. She stood there listening. A long time passed before the truck's engine finally roared. She went to the door and opened it wide, watching brick-red dust billow in the Silverado's wake. Pangs of regret kicked around in her stomach as Clay drove off.

And a question kept popping into her head, begging to be answered.

Had she made a big mistake coming back to Worth Ranch?

Clay drank a big gulp of Jack Daniel's, aiming to numb his senses. The alcohol scorched sliding down and he relished the quick burn. He was getting everything he wanted, wasn't he? A divorce from Trish and a willing woman in Suzy Johnson. Suzy wasn't complicated. She knew exactly what she wanted—him. She hadn't come right out and said that, but Clay figured as much. Since her divorce from a loser husband, they'd resumed their lifelong friendship and she'd hinted that she wanted to get much closer. Suzy was a woman he could build a life with and raise a family, so why the hell was he holding back?

He sat on the steps of Tagg's porch, stretching out and swirling the amber liquid in his glass.

"You want to tell me why you popped over here?" Tagg said, sipping Coors from the bottle, sitting right next to him.

"Can't a guy visit his brother?"

Tagg laughed and Clay grazed him with a look. "Right. Now you've taken to coming all the way up to my house for a visit. When you saw me just fine today at Penny's Song."

Tagg's newly built house sat on the original location of Worth Ranch, with a spectacular view of the Red Ridge Mountain range. Clay shrugged a shoulder and took another swig. "I didn't feel like drinking alone."

"Uh-huh. You didn't stay long at the campfire with the kids."

"I went to Suzy's. Her dad was visiting and he wanted to talk to me about that old bull, Razor. I think he was craving male company. Suzy's got her place looking like a flower festival gone bad."

Tagg laughed. "How's ole Quinn doing?"

Suzy's father had been Rory Worth's best friend. Through the years, the two cronies told some wild stories about their youth. They'd been tossed in jail half a dozen times before they'd wised up and got serious about the cattle business.

"Getting old and repeating the same stories over and over but I never tire of hearing 'em. He's still cantankerous as ever, though, so he can't be too bad off."

"Yeah, well, that's good. Suzy make pie?" Tagg asked with longing in his voice.

"Cherry."

"Oh, man."

Everybody in Red Ridge knew Suzy made award-winning cherry pie. If they'd been fortunate enough to taste it, they were hooked. She took the prize every year at the county fair.

"You didn't stay long…at Suzy's."

Clay gave Tagg a sidelong look. He lifted his tumbler, looking through the beveled glass to the last gulp of whiskey inside. "She wasn't serving what I needed."

Tagg smiled. "You mean to say, she wasn't Trish. Your wife shows up and all of a sudden Suzy's pie doesn't taste so good."

"I never said that."

"But Trish is on your mind."

"I married her, Tagg. Hell, yeah. She's on my mind. I thought maybe once, something with Trish would be simple. Easy, you know. Talk over terms, sign the divorce papers and move on with our lives. But she shows up here with a kid."

"Must've been quite a shock."

Clay shook his head in disbelief. It had been the last thing he'd expected. "What did Dad always say? Could've knocked me over with a feather."

"That baby is really cute," Tagg said. "Callie went on and on about her today."

"Yeah, she's…beautiful." Clay rubbed the back of his neck. "Truth is, the situation isn't anybody's fault. Trish did what needed doing regarding Meggie. I don't fault her that."

"Generous of you."

Clay sent his brother a glare. "What's that supposed to mean?"

"You're holding a grudge against her…I can see it in your eyes."

"You don't know jack."

Tagg lifted the bottle to his lips. "Clay, no offense, but you're a bear when you don't get your way." He took a swallow, then went on, "The way I see it, Trish was the first woman who didn't fawn all over you and lay a red carpet at your feet. She didn't give up everything to be with you. She made you work. It's probably why you fell so hard for her in the first place."

Clay pursed his lips. Tagg was forgetting Trish walked out on him. He'd never told his brothers about her accusations, though, how she hadn't trusted him. How she believed he'd cheated on her with Suzy. "You taking her side?"

Tagg inhaled sharply. "Nope, I'm just trying to put things in perspective."

"Like I can't do that myself?" Clay's annoyance rang in the pitch of his voice.

"I'm just saying."

"Lay off, okay?"

"Sure thing. I'll lay off you the way you laid off me when it came to Callie."

Clay's mouth twisted with smug certainty. "I was right about Callie."

Tagg didn't deny it. "Yeah, you were."

Satisfaction curved Clay's lips up until Tagg laid a hand on his shoulder and gave him a look of brotherly concern. "Sometimes, we can't see what's right in front of us."

Clay scowled and finished off his whiskey. He handed his brother the empty glass. "Thanks for the double shot and the *sermon*."

He rose and ignored Tagg's innocent expression. "You're leaving already?"

Clay lifted his eyes heavenward. "Do me a favor, go inside to your wife."

"Maybe you should do the same," Tagg said and before Clay could tear him a new one, Tagg skedaddled into the house, the screen door flapping twice before settling closed.

Clay strung out a line of curses all the way to his truck. When he got in, seeing the empty car seat in the back of the cab knotted his stomach. Meggie's sweet baby scent permeated the air, a combination of formula and those handy wipes mixed in with the scent of fresh cotton. He'd been aware of the car seat before and made a mental note to have Wes drop it off to Trish in the morning along with the car keys to her old Volvo. But right now, with nothing but a starless lonely night to look forward to, when he allowed himself to feel, a deep hollow ache bruised his gut. His life hadn't turned out as he'd hoped. By now, he should have had two car seats filled with toddlers and a loving wife by his side. It wasn't Rory's wish any longer, it was Clay's, and it was high time he did something about it.

A man could do worse than hooking up with a friendly woman who could bake her way into heaven's gates. Hell, Trish had been right today. It was time to finalize their divorce. He needed to get his life rolling again. Make babies. Raise a family.

Start living again.

Trish hadn't been stood up since her freshman year in high school.

But here she was waiting on a man who hadn't shown.

Clay missed their appointment. Trish went over the brief conversation they'd had about it yesterday. She was certain Clay said he'd come by at four o'clock today—she hadn't heard wrong. She glanced at the digital clock on the oven. It was nearly quarter to five.

She paced the kitchen floor and every so often she'd walk over to the front window to peek outside for some sign of him. He hadn't been thrilled when she'd brought up the divorce, but it had to be done. And frankly, after he'd received the phone call from Suzy, Trish saw no need in waiting. It was a good part of the reason she'd returned to Worth Ranch. Once they came to terms, she could devote her time and skill to the fundraiser and then be gone. She had a business to run, a child to care for and she had to figure out a way to make it all work somehow. Her *life* was back in Nashville now.

"Where the heck is he?" she asked Meggie.

The baby sat upright on a quilt, entertained by a Disney music box that played "It's a Small World after All" over and over again. The tune was embedded in Trish's brain, but the toy kept the baby quietly amused, so she endured it.

At the very least, Clay could have called. Fifteen minutes ago, she'd tried his cell and gotten his voice mail. It was dinnertime. She couldn't put off Meggie's meal any longer. She opened a box of rice cereal and poured a couple of teaspoons into a plastic bowl and was just about to pour formula into the mix when the doorbell chimed.

"Finally," she said, wiping her hands on her jeans. She didn't know if she was annoyed that Clay had shown up late or relieved that he'd shown up at all. "Come with me, sweet baby." She swept Meggie up in her arms and walked toward the entrance.

She opened the door to find Clay's housekeeper on her porch. "Oh. Hello, Helen."

"Hello, Mrs. Worth." Frown lines arched the older woman's mouth downward.

"I was expecting Clay," Trish said, surprised that she wasn't seeing her soon-to-be ex on the doorstep.

"I know. He sent me over. Clay was in a car accident coming home from Phoenix this afternoon."

The look on Helen's face worried her. Trish's breath froze in her chest as dozens of horrifying images popped in her head. "Is he—"

"He'll be fine," Helen said carefully. "I think he's more irritated than anything else. Someone ran a red light and plowed into his car."

"Oh, no."

"He got shaken up a bit. The airbag saved him from serious injury. It's a good thing his brother Jackson was nearby. He's with Clay now."

"Where are they?"

"Jackson's making him see the doctor in Phoenix." Helen's sullen face brightened a little. "He wasn't happy about it. I haven't heard such language coming out of that boy's mouth since his father took his car away when he was sixteen."

Trish didn't smile at the notion. "But he's going to be okay, right?"

Helen nodded slowly, but it was clear that this news had shaken her, too. "He was lucky. So was the driver of the other car. He had minor injuries, too. It could have been a good deal worse. I'm very thankful."

"Me, too." She was floored and a little baffled by the news. "Well, I certainly didn't expect this."

"No, life has a way of happening all around you."

The sadness in her tone reminded Trish about the way Helen had lost her husband. He'd died years ago in a major pileup on the highway, when a semi truck fishtailed off the road. There'd been seven fatalities—seven lives taken and dozens upon dozens of hearts broken that day.

"Clay will be home later. He said he'd call you." Helen's eyes drifted to Meggie. "How's she doing?"

She gave Meggie a squeeze, bringing her closer. "She's doing better than I… Helen, why don't you come inside? I was just about to feed her."

A smile graced the woman's face and it was obvious she could use some company. She loved the Worth boys like her own, but she'd been closer to Clay than any of them. "Maybe for a minute or two."

"I'll make tea. I've got lemon chamomile. Good for the nerves."

Helen followed her into the kitchen. "Don't let me be a bother. Go ahead and feed the baby first."

"Oh, well. I haven't put the high chair together yet." The box was halfway open on the floor by the sliding glass door in the back. "I usually feed her on my lap. I mean, I just now started giving her something more solid. The pediatrician said her appetite was growing and it was fine to give her a little supplement."

"You're making pablum?"

"Yeah, I guess that's what it's called. Meggie loves it."

"Will she come to me?" Helen reached her arms out. "I'll hold her while you feed her."

"Thank you." Cautiously, she set the baby in Helen's arms. Trish could tell she was a grandmother with loads of experience handling children. The baby took right to her and settled comfortably as she sat at the wrought iron-and-glass table. Helen made funny sounds and gestures to amuse the baby. Meggie looked on with curious awe and her sweet expression calmed Trish's fragile nerves. Her heart had leaped in her chest when she thought Clay might have been injured. Too many feelings emerged and the weight they carried frightened her.

"She's really a good baby," Trish said, bringing the mixture over and sitting down beside them.

"That she is," Helen agreed.

After they fed Meggie and put her down in the play yard that Trish had struggled to assemble, Helen helped her get the high chair set up. The woman was a wiz with baby equipment and zipped through the assembly process in short time.

Trish asked Helen to stay for dinner. She made a chicken avocado salad and during the meal, they spoke of family and friends. Helen had a genuine giving nature, although she'd been guarded with Trish during her marriage to Clay. Now, it seemed Helen was friendlier and more open in her conversation. They discussed favorite television shows, the best baby buys and then Helen caught her up on Red Ridge gossip. Of course she refrained from saying that Trish coming back to Red Ridge had been the lead topic of conversation. Clay was the homegrown favorite son—the superstar who had the heart of a cowboy. The townsfolk loved that Clay had retired to his Red Ridge ranch, so naturally the return of his estranged wife was big news.

It was eight o'clock when Helen left the house. With all the afternoon stimulation, it had been a breeze getting Meggie to sleep. She slept on her back in the crib dressed in a light green SleepSack decorated with pink roses. Trish gently turned her head to the side, facing the wall.

"No flat-head syndrome for you, sweet baby," she whispered, brushing an air kiss over her hair. Babies slept on their backs these days with their faces turned to the side. It amazed Trish just how much she'd had to learn. In those first few weeks, she'd made a record amount of phone calls to the pediatrician.

She walked into the shower, stripped out of her clothes and let the warm soothing water caress her tired body. The soaking felt good right down to her toes and eased her tight muscles. When she got out, she dried her hair and then dressed in her most comfy nightclothes, a pair of gray cut-off sweats and a soft cotton T-shirt that was fraying around the collar.

She picked up yet another how-to baby book and sat down on the sofa, propping her feet under her. She didn't get more than a page read when a soft knocking on the front door interrupted her. She closed the book and rose, mindful of the time. It was almost nine o'clock. She could only think of one person who would show up here this late.

She padded with bare feet to the entrance and opened the door. When she saw him standing on her doorstep, a bruise on his cheekbone in varying stages of purple and a bandage on his wrist, concern registered first. Her mouth opened and then shut when she met his eyes. Flutters of awareness zipped through her body like a powerful, bone-melting force of nature.

Wordless, he took all of her in, his gaze achingly slow, roaming over her body with an incendiary look that fired her blood. No other man could look at her like that and cause such a reaction. His eyes were red-hot pokers, searing her when they touched her breasts, her belly and *below*. She'd forgotten she'd come to the door dressed in flimsy nightclothes.

The burning hunger in his eyes reminded her.

Under his scrutiny, her nipples pebbled, which only made matters worse.

Heart thrumming against her chest, she whispered a breath. "Clay."

Four

Clay stood on Trish's porch and forgot about the accident that totaled his car. He forgot about the ache in his ribs, the soreness in his arm and the damn bruises on his face. The second he laid eyes on his wife, blood pounded in his head—the throbbing having nothing to do with his head injury.

She came to the door wearing nothing much of anything, her long legs exposed in cutoffs that barely covered the tops of her thighs. He'd remembered how they'd felt under his palms, soft and creamy, just the way they looked now. There wasn't anything about Trish's body he'd forgotten. His gaze moved up to breasts barely concealed by thin cotton. Each rounded globe was visible, with a darkened protrusion at the center, the hard tips stretching the material. His blood stirred. Heat pulsed through his body like wildfire.

The expression on her face matched his, pure, unabashed sexual frustration. He wasn't the only one feeling the torture of yearlong celibacy.

There...there hasn't been anyone else.

Her words had brought him relief and satisfaction.

"What are...how are you?" she stammered, drawing her lower lip in with her teeth. Fear entered her eyes, but not the kind that would have her running away. This fear was just what he'd hoped for. Fear of the inevitable. "I was just going to bed."

He smiled and saw Trish break out in goose bumps. It was his cue to enter the house. He brushed past her and turned, waiting for her to close the door. She hesitated and he got a good look at her from the backside. The shorts crept up the back of her thighs and the bottom edge of two perfect cheeks peeked out from the ragged sweats she wore. Two handfuls of heaven. Clay's breath caught in his throat. He swallowed down the raw lust that threatened to consume him. Hell, his wife looked like every man's fantasy, an Ellie Mae Clampett of modern times.

Trish whirled around to face him and he got a whiff of citrus and shampoo. Saw a pretty face washed clean of the day, blue summer-sky eyes and long blond hair curling at the ends. She stood by the door, her eyes fluttering, darting away.

"Come here, Trish."

Her eyes slammed shut and she gave a little shake of her head.

"Come," he rasped, the demand emanating from a dark forbidden place.

Her eyes opened and slowly she moved toward him, shaking her head. "This isn't a good idea."

When she reached him, he grabbed her wrists and pulled her up close until she was pressed against him. He wrapped his arms around her waist, her breasts crushed to his chest. He ignored the pain shooting from his ribs, but the ache below his waist he couldn't ignore. "Tell me when you think of a better one."

With a smooth stroke, he tilted her chin up and lowered his head down. His lips brushed hers gently, the kiss an open invitation and Trish welcomed him by responding without resistance. Sweet like sugar and familiar like morning coffee, Clay couldn't forget her taste.

She pulled away slightly, as far as he would let her. Her eyes searched his with deep concern. Her hand came up to the bruise on his face and she caressed him with tenderness. "You're hurt."

"I'll live."

"But you—"

He kissed away her worries and then deepened the kiss. She whimpered from deep inside her throat. Clay cursed. His willpower vanished. He kissed her urgently now, parting her lips, his tongue filling the sweet hollow of her mouth. She moaned and fell into his kisses, scrambling for a way to get closer. Clay brought her up, rubbing his erection to her groin. Hell, she felt good. She moved against him in a rhythmic grind, teasing him with her hot little body, just the way he loved.

"Make another one of those little sounds of yours," his voice scraped out low, "and I swear to you, it'll be over before it starts."

With a coy smile, her eyes gleamed with hunger, tempting him with raised brows even though she didn't make a sound. She stood before him and he backed away slightly. He took hold of her T-shirt with both hands at her waist and, too damn impatient to be smooth, he yanked it up and over her head. Her breasts bobbed from the pull and he sucked in oxygen watching them settle onto her chest. He stared at their perfection, round and full with pink tips that pointed heavenward.

"Holy hell." The air left his lungs. They weren't three feet into the doorway and she had him hard and ready to sweep them into oblivion.

"Take your shorts off," he commanded with urgency.

"Your shirt first," she countered, her breath coming out in a rush.

He wouldn't take his shirt off. Not until they were in the dark. He wouldn't let her see his battered chest. If she did, she'd send him home to rest. It was the last thing he needed tonight.

He sent her a sly smile. "Never mind, I have a better idea." He drew her close again and turned her around, so that her back pressed against his chest.

Adjusting her position, he settled behind her and cupped her breasts. They were firm and sensitive to his touch. His need intensified. His erection against her backside, barely restrained by his jeans, Clay inhaled her erotic scent. "I have good ideas. Admit it."

He kissed her soft throat and then moved farther down to scrape his teeth over her shoulders.

"Mmm."

He closed his eyes to the pleasure, weighing the soft round mounds in his hands, playing her like an instrument. She moaned with each flick of his thumbs. Cried out with each gentle pinch of his fingers. He palmed her and filled his hands, caressing her with gentleness first, then stroking her nipples with rough quick strokes.

He ached to be inside her. To feel her warmth and heat surround him. To make them both come undone with a powerful release.

Gripping her arm with one hand, he slid the other hand down along her torso, past her flat belly and farther yet over her navel. He slipped his hand under her shorts, the sweatshirt material easily giving way. He felt her softness, the curls that protected her, and he wove his fingers through them as he shoved her panties to the side. Teasing her with his fingertips, edging closer, her anticipation grew. Her body stilled.

She drew a sharp breath. The arch of her hips as she leaned her head against his shoulder invited him in.

He dipped his finger and stroked soft flesh. "Damn, Trish. Honey, you're wet for me already."

A shudder ran through her and she made a tiny little noise, a gasp of a sound.

He found patience somehow, tempting her with slow strokes, one, then another and another, each deliberate, each leading to something more potent, each with the intent to bring her the greatest pleasure.

"Please, Clay," she whispered, moving against him, his body taking the force of her gyrations against his swollen groin. "I need…"

His fingers slid over her again and again, stronger, more purposeful now. He knew what Trish liked. He knew her body best. And when she uttered quick sharp cries, her hips frantic, her body quivering with hot flames, her release came hard and fast. Shudders racked her body in waves and waves. She succumbed to them, feeling taut against him at first, then her limbs became loose as the tremors took over. The way she climaxed, giving in to a full powerful orgasm, turned Clay inside out. His body was ready to burst. He held her upright where her knees might have caved, cradling her against him.

"You have good ideas," she muttered on a soft, sated breath.

Gently, he turned her around. The fire in her eyes was there, still burning hot. She answered his question before he asked.

"Meggie is sleeping in the crib."

Clay grabbed her hand and led her to the other bedroom where only a hint of moonlight streamed in. They stopped by the side of the bed. He drew her close and crushed a kiss to her lips. "Get naked."

This time she didn't argue. She shimmied out of her shorts and her pink bikini panties. Moonlight paled her skin. She was an ethereal beauty with flowing hair and a curvaceous body. He drank in the sight of her as he sat down and yanked off his boots. She came to him then, half helping, half fumbling with the removal of his clothes. He plucked a condom out of his pants pocket and Trish's expression changed. She took the packet out of his hand and stared at it, ready to say something.

Clay grabbed hold of her wrists and leaned back on the bed, pulling her with him. She toppled a little and then righted herself on her knees, straddling him like she would a wild stallion, her body lording over him.

"I carry them, just in case," he explained.

"And how many *cases* have there been?" she whispered.

Clay pursed his lips. She had a right to know the truth, but he didn't want a discussion right now, with his brain functioning south of his waistline. "Okay, I'll admit it. I put them in my pocket tonight. Before I walked over here."

"Because?"

He was hoping to get lucky with his wife? Because he'd wanted her the second she'd stepped out of that taxi the other day. "Right after I realized I wasn't going to die today, I thought of you."

"I was your first thought?"

"Yeah," he admitted, his lips curving up. He'd imagined her just like this.

He didn't want to dwell on the ramifications of that right now. The minute after the airbag deployed and he realized his body parts were still working on all cylinders, Trish's image had popped into his head. Out of the blue. He'd blamed it on the concussion, this complete loss of wits, yet here she was, naked and beautiful, just like the visual he'd had of her, and Clay figured luck was with him today, in more ways than one.

His erection was killing him. Then a smile brightened her wary features and she stroked his chest, tempting him like a she-devil. "Well, cowboy, what are you waiting for?" She handed him a condom.

Clay growled and made quick work of securing it. "You're gonna be sorry you said that."

"I hope so."

He gripped her hips splaying his hands wide, just as she rose, and together they fitted her onto his thick shaft, two parts of a puzzle interlocking at the end of a yearlong dry patch.

Sensations ripped through him as he entered her with a thrust that was months in the making. She was tight and wet and she made him sweat just by looking at her—her head thrown back, her eyes closed—absorbing him without a shred of hesitation. She offered no resistance at all.

Clay arched up. Holding on to her hips as levers for pleasure, he guided her down with measured, torturous force, until he reached the ultimate limits of her body. She moaned and whipped her head forward, her expression shock and awe under the moon's soft glow.

Clay met with her eyes, dark midnight blue sparks igniting. And the fire within him continued to burn. She moved. He moved. They were one with the universe shifting to accommodate each other's needs.

Aching and ready for wild release, Clay brought her down to him, their bodies flush. Her arms came around his neck. He kissed her thoroughly, completely, then rolled her over until she was under him on the sheets. She was petite yet strong, but he held his body back for fear of hurting her. He gripped the bedpost for support and shook the damn thing near to breaking as he drove his body to the edge. Trish followed his lead, moving underneath him, turning him inside out with her little gasps of tormented delight. His body was racked, his willpower gone. He needed this moment, this release. It had been too damn long.

"Come with me," he gritted out as his pace quickened, his body reaching an unmatched crescendo.

Trish surrendered, her body giving way to trembles of pleasure. He felt the exact moment when her orgasm hit, the waves like little earthquakes bursting forth and it was all he needed. He came hard. With potent force. He pumped out his frustration, shed his unwanted celibacy and fulfilled raw sexual need. His groans were met with the cries. Together they blended into one with a last shred of energy.

Clay's heartbeats pounded in his head.

He stilled and waited for his breath to return to somewhat normal, then looked down at Trish. Sated, she had a beautiful glow, but her body was limp as a rag doll.

"Are you sure you were in an accident today?" she murmured, spent.

He smiled and rolled onto his back. "I've got the concussion to prove it."

She gasped and turned to him. "Tell me, you really don't."

"I do." With a cunning look, he met her gaze and added, "The doctor said I shouldn't be alone tonight."

As Clay slept beside her, Trish looked over his body and shuddered when she thought of him being in a head-on collision. Aside from bruises on his face and a cut over his left eye, making him look somewhat dashing, his chest was black and blue in several places with varying degrees of discolor. Now, she understood why he wouldn't allow her to undress him until they were under the cover of darkness in the bedroom. If she'd seen the road map of pain on his body she would have sent him away to rest and recuperate.

Earlier when she'd opened the door to him, she hadn't

cared why he'd come. She'd been greatly relieved he was alive and she'd forgotten they were on the precipice of divorce.

Then Clay had seduced her with a deadly smile and the temptation of sexual bliss. But Trish wasn't the victim in this. She wouldn't blame him. She'd been an oh-so-willing partner. She'd wanted him the second she'd seen him standing on her doorstep.

Sex had been missing in her life lately.

And Clay was the sexiest man she'd ever met.

She wouldn't read more into what happened. If Clay's claims were true, then he'd gone without sex for months, too, and that's what last night had amounted to—a need to satisfy sexual craving.

She touched the hair at the nape of his neck, playing with a strand that curled up and around her finger, and wondered if it could be that easy. Could she rationalize this with her analytical mind and come to that conclusion? It was all about sex. Clay knew her body like no other man. He knew what she liked, how she wanted to be touched. He'd always been an expert lover.

Her body had splintered, more than once, and the peace that settled around her, the completion she felt wasn't a small thing.

Clay stirred and Trish quickly removed her hand from his neck.

She laid there, content in the aftermath of lovemaking for a time, closing her eyes and listening to his quiet breathing. When she heard Meggie's morning complaint, a sound she was becoming more and more familiar with, she rose quietly. Slipping on her robe, she stole a glance at Clay. She still couldn't believe he was in her bed. He'd confessed to having a concussion, *after* they'd made love. Nothing stopped Clay when he wanted something and even though he'd been reckless with his injuries, she was grateful he was strong and healthy. Still, she'd watched him half the night, despite his claims to feeling fine.

A concussion wasn't something to mess with.

She padded into the master bedroom. A night-light sent soft beams over the crib and haloed Meggie in a circle of light. She was waking. It was nearly dawn and this had been her pattern, to wake for a short time and then fall back asleep for a few hours.

Trish had been on the baby's schedule for weeks now and tried to adjust, although singing songs, reading the ABC book and squeezing squeak toys hadn't been on her list of favorite things to do at the crack of dawn.

"How's my little sweet pea this morning?"

Meggie stared at her, her blue eyes wide and filled with mischief. She opened her mouth babbling incoherent sounds that someday would form into her first real words.

"That good?" she asked, reaching down to pick up the baby. "Let's get you a clean diaper."

A dim sliver of light rose on the horizon, and after Trish diapered the baby, she walked her over to the parlor window to gaze outside. It was a sweet time of day, holding a child in her arms, watching the sublime rising of the sun. "See that?" she said softly. "Say, sun."

Meggie followed the direction of her pointing finger and cooed and ahhed. Trish repeated. "Sun."

The baby gazed at her quizzically. She was trying, Trish noted.

She lingered by the window for a time, enjoying the view until Meggie squirmed uncomfortably. It was time for a feeding; the baby was getting hungry. She walked into the kitchen and pulled a bottle filled with formula out of the refrigerator. "Breakfast."

Trish walked into the parlor and sat on the sofa. She

propped Meggie up on her lap and brought the bottle to her mouth. "Here you go."

The baby cupped both hands around the bottle, touching Trish's fingers, and took a sip. A loud cry rang out and Meggie backed her head away, her lips pulling down, and tears beginning to fall. It only took a second to realize why the baby was crying.

"Oh, shoot! I'm sorry. I'm so sorry, Meggie."

Trish rose and turned, bumping smack into Clay. He grabbed her arms to steady her and glanced at the fitful baby, who was still crying. "What's wrong?"

Sleep-tousled, with morning scruff on his face and hair jutting out in three different directions, Clay oozed *sexy* without even trying. "I forgot to warm up her bottle. It's ice-cold."

"Let me have her," Clay said. "Go heat the bottle."

Trish hesitated for half a second, but Clay's arms came out and Meggie, the traitor, went right into them. He held her cautiously, bringing her close to his chest. "Go," he said, letting her know by his tone he knew what he was doing.

It was obvious for all her smarts, book learning and gallant effort, she didn't know what the heck *she* was doing. This wasn't the first time she'd forgotten to heat Meggie's bottle. She took the cold bottle and admonished herself all the way to the kitchen.

It wasn't the end of the world, but she should have remembered. She couldn't blame it on Clay's presence in the house either, or the mind-numbing sex she'd just had. The early hour was out, as an excuse. She was up this early every morning. She heated the bottle in a pan of hot water and noted that Meggie's crying had stopped.

Minutes later, after making sure the temperature was just right Trish walked back into the parlor. She found Meggie on Clay's lap, playing with her favorite toy, the zoo piano. The sight of the two of them, heads together, intent on spinning the lion's mane and jiggling the giraffe's neck up and down was enough to bring tears to Trish's eyes.

Dejected, she took a seat on the sofa, the bottle between her legs on her lap.

"It's no big deal," Clay said, sparing her a glance. "Don't be so hard on yourself."

"I get frustrated."

Clay kept his focus on Meggie. The two of them looked perfect together. "You think biological mothers don't make mistakes? You think they do everything right?"

Trish sighed deep in her throat. "No, but—"

Meggie lunged forward and pressed her little hand on the piano keys. Lights blinked on and off and she chuckled as the notes rang out a melodious tune. "She really likes this thing," Clay said.

"It's her favorite toy."

"She loves music. I should play guitar for her sometime."

Trish's heart warmed at Clay's tone. "She's got rhythm."

Clay nodded. "Yeah."

"I should probably feed her. She should go back to sleep for a while."

Clay set the zoo piano aside and turned Meggie toward Trish. As soon as the baby saw the bottle, she leaned forward and nearly jumped out of Clay's lap. "See, all is forgiven and forgotten."

Trish didn't know about that. She struggled with the small things. She wondered how she'd handle the bigger things when the time came. She'd rather deal with a spoiled movie actor after a career-sucking scandal than make any more mistakes with Meggie.

Clay sat with Trish while she fed Meggie. He leaned back against the sofa cushions with his eyes closed.

"You're tired," she said. "You should go to bed."

Clay didn't open his eyes, but a smile graced his bruised face. "I was thinking the same thing about you."

Trish inhaled a deep breath. So that was it? It was just about sex.

"How long before she falls asleep?"

"Meggie? Oh, I don't know. A couple of minutes. Her eyes are closing with each sip." Meggie had sucked the bottle down to an inch of formula.

Clay rose. "Okay, I'll meet you back in bed in a few."

Trish's brows lifted and her heart strummed with panic. "You're going back to…to that bed?"

He nodded and looked at her, confused. "Where else?"

"Clay, we should talk about what happened last night."

He leaned over and landed a sweeping kiss on her lips. "We will. In bed. I'm going to take a rest. Don't be long." He gave her a wink, patted Meggie's head ever so gently and then was gone.

Fifteen minutes later after putting a sleeping Meggie down into her crib, Trish bolstered her courage. She had to speak with Clay, but she wouldn't deny she was on shaky footing here. Once, she'd loved Clay to distraction, but now she had a baby to consider and a life in Nashville that she'd built for herself.

She entered the smaller bedroom, walking in quietly. Clay was lying on his back, his hands behind his head with eyes closed, probably asleep. Good. Problem solved. She could leave him in peace. She would let him get the rest he obviously needed. On tiptoes, she turned to leave. "Don't go."

"Oh!" Startled, she stammered, "I, uh, thought you were resting."

He sent her a killer smile. "I was. Waiting for you."

"Why?" Oh, man. Had she actually asked him that? She only had to look at the hunger in his eyes to know the answer.

He bounded up from the bed and her gaze flew straight to the tight bulge protruding from his black boxer briefs. She took a big swallow and knew what was on his mind. He moved like a sleek lazy cat coming toward her. She'd forgotten how commanding he was in the buff. What a beautiful body he had, despite the bruising that tainted his skin. Now, it seemed to add to his primal appeal. Clay came closer. "You're not really asking me *why,* are you?"

She bit her lower lip, then moistened it with a stroke of her tongue.

The gesture didn't go unnoticed. One brow arched up as he stepped closer, stalking her. "Clay, last night was—"

He stopped a foot away and pulled the tie of her fluffy white robe. She closed her eyes as the material spread open and even without bearing witness, she felt the smoldering heat of his gaze as he perused her naked body.

"Don't complicate things, honey."

With nimble, practiced fingers, he shed the material from her shoulders and when the robe fell to the floor, Clay inhaled a sharp breath. Her eyes opened to his burning gaze. His voice hoarse, he said, "You're beautiful and my wife for a little while longer."

She couldn't deny their marital status. She was his wife. Not that she owed him sex, but she wasn't a fool either. Clay knew how to make her come apart at the seams and she'd missed that. She'd missed making love. "Are you suggesting we have unfinished business?" she asked in barely a whisper.

He took another step closer. Goose bumps rose on her arms. Had it just been a few hours since they'd made love? She was coming undone all over again. He pressed his body to hers ever so slightly, his strong chest against the upended tips of her nipples. The friction made her squirm below the waist.

His face went tight, his eyes darkened to searing-hot coals.

The heady force of his sex pressed into hers and flames ignited inside her body.

"I'm saying, we have unfinished *pleasure*."

He scraped out the word, making it seem dirty, lusty and sensual as hell. She nodded silently, holding on to that truth. Her body needed his. They had months of catching up to do.

When she thought he'd lead her over to the bed, he lifted her instead and set her on the top edge of the dresser. The cool polished wood met with her derriere and an incredible thrill shot through her. He rid himself of his briefs. With a kick, they went flying. Bending his head, he kissed her thoroughly on the lips. His tongue sought entrance to the deep recesses of her mouth and she opened for him. She met him stroke for stroke, open-mouthed and wild until they were nearly breathless.

Clay cupped her legs and wrapped them around his waist. She hung on, tightening herself around him like a bow on a Christmas gift. With a growl of impatience, he lifted her from behind, his big hands squeezing her cheeks for stability and positioning himself with a pulsing erection that teased the very tip of her womanhood. Trish's mind melted and her anticipation grew.

Clay didn't waste time. He immediately drove himself deep and pumped into her. With a groan of satisfaction, he murmured. "So damn good."

She hung on to his neck, bowing her body, meeting his thrusts, his hands pressing her closer, closer still. She felt her own explosion, waves upon waves of hot scorching jolts, careening her into a state of frenzied pleasure. She cried out his name, huffing short little breaths until the last wave consumed her.

Clay's release came right after in long, full, powerful gyrations that popped veins on his neck and made him wince with the potency of his dazzling release. He made primitive sounds, a gushing of words that poured out of him like a rushing river.

When they were spent, he lowered her down along his body, holding her tight. He kissed her hair, her throat and then her mouth gently. "Trish," he said with a gravelly voice and then was silent.

Trish felt the same way. There weren't words.

Clay took her hand and guided her back to bed silently. When they were both tucked in, he brought his body close, curving her into the contours of his frame. His warmth seeped in, his breaths fanned her nape and the quiet in the house soothed them into a calming sleep.

Trish stood at the coffeemaker, waiting for Mr. Coffee to serve up enough caffeine to jolt her mind back into reality. She couldn't believe what happened between her and Clay last night and then again in the wee hours of the morning. How had she let it go so far?

Reality sucked, was her father's favorite saying.

Yes, damn it. It did.

She had more than a few realities to deal with this morning. First, she relished the relief her body felt. Months and months of pent-up frustration had been wiped clean with just a few hours of making love with Clay. Her body hummed. Sated and complete, she felt light as air, as though she could dance on the clouds. She hadn't realized how much she'd missed having sex with Clay, having him complement her body, kiss every hollow and caress her most intimate areas until she cried out from tormented pleasure. Hot shivers rushed through her body thinking about how he'd taken her last night.

But reality did suck because in the light of day, Trish came to some tough conclusions. She couldn't allow what happened last night with Clay to ever happen again. She was here on the ranch for one main reason: to shed her past and begin her life as a single mother. She had a daughter to raise to adulthood and Meggie's wants and needs had to come first. It was essential not to blow this chance.

The way your mother did with you.

Trish loved her mother, flighty as she was, but knew in her heart that her relationship with Meggie would be a hundred times better. Alicia Fontaine had tried but not hard enough. Not long enough. She'd had her hands full with Blake and she'd barely been able to cope. There hadn't been anything left for a daughter who'd desperately wanted a morsel of her mother's attention. Trish felt guilty that she'd been jealous of Blake, sick as he was for most of his childhood, because he'd been nurtured and doted upon, while she'd been left to fend for herself.

How many school open houses had her mother missed? How many culminations and awards ceremonies? Almost all of them, from what Trish could recall, which made her protective of Meggie in too many ways to name.

She couldn't afford to let Meggie get close to Clay. It would be cruel and serve no purpose to allow the baby to form any kind of attachment to him. Trish was leaving soon. She and Clay had no future together. The child had lost her father already. She'd been ripped out of her mother's arms by Karin's untimely death. The baby had enough adjustments to make and as inept a mother as Trish was, she was all Meggie had now. It wouldn't be fair to Meggie to allow her to bond with Clay.

The pungent aroma of French roast filled the kitchen. The drip, drip, drip stopped as steam rose with a hiss from the coffeemaker. Trish poured a cup for herself, staring at the simmering pot, deep in thought.

"Got another one of those?"

Her breath caught as Clay came up behind her and circled

his arms around her waist. The deep rich timbre of his voice created tingles. Vivid memories of what they'd done together on and *off* the bed last night flashed in her head. Now, she found it difficult not to lean against his strong shoulders and press her head to his chest. Absorb his strength and give herself up to him for these few early dawn moments.

"Oh, uh, sure. I'll pour you some."

He stuck his nose into her hair and breathed her in. "You smell good. You showered already, without me?"

Oh, boy. Even though he tried to sound hurt, she knew he was teasing. That didn't prevent more images from popping into her head. Steam and heat made for memorable times in the shower with Clay.

Back in Nashville, her mission had been clear and the thought of seeing Clay again hadn't hindered her determination. But now that she was here, seeing him in the flesh, literally, things were getting very complicated. She couldn't afford that. At this point in her life more than any other time, Trish needed *simple*. They still had to discuss the divorce, but not today. Today she had to focus on the fundraiser. "I've got work to do today for Penny's Song." She turned, handing him a cup of coffee. "Here you go."

Clay took the coffee and sat on the stool opposite her at the granite island, watching her as he sipped. He sensed her mood—she saw it in the way his eyes followed her. "Meggie still asleep?"

Trish inhaled. "Yes. If I'm lucky, I'll get my coffee down before she wakes up." She sent him a small smile.

Clay had showered and dressed in the clothes he'd worn last night. In the daylight, without night shadows giving him a harsher appearance, his face looked better, although he was still bruised. She'd kissed the cut above his eye last night and he told her she'd cured him. When Clay was charming like that, Trish had little defense against him.

"I've got a full day. Going to have to deal with the accident today, and get a new car."

"Your car was *totaled?*" This was news she hadn't heard and it surprised her. When Clay wasn't using the truck, he drove a Mercedes.

"Yeah. The driver was just under the legal alcohol limit."

"Oh, wow." How close he'd come to losing his life. He'd been fortunate to walk away with minor injuries. A shudder ran through her at the thought.

"So I was thinking, how about I bring over dinner later tonight?"

It sounded like heaven, a quiet dinner with Clay. But her nerves jangled and more resolute, rational thoughts broke free. Being the adult wasn't fun. She'd been the responsible one all of her life, today being no different.

"Clay, it's not a good idea."

A slow, easy grin spread across his face. "I thought I had *good* ideas. You said so yourself about a dozen times last night." He took a sip of coffee, amusement reaching his eyes.

Trish squelched those images. His *ideas* had given her mind-blowing orgasms and a night she'd never forget, but morning brought her sanity back. "Last night was incredible," she said honestly, on a rushed breath. "I'm not sorry, it's something we both wanted and needed, but we can't—"

"Why not?" Clay set his cup down carefully and pierced her with a stern look. "Why *can't* we?"

"Because it's pointless."

He hesitated for a moment, as if she'd surprised him, then he shook his head. "Don't analyze it, Trish. We're still married."

For the next few weeks. "Well, I can't separate the two in my head. I can't make love with you and pretend we're not split up. I can't do that to myself or to Meggie. She's already lost so much. I can't allow her to lose anything more."

Clay rose from the seat. His chest filled with oxygen, not in an imposing way, but as if simply trying to figure her out. "What is she going to lose if I come over for dinner?"

Trish held her ground, although inside she felt torn between wanting him and pushing him away. Either way, she'd come out the loser. "It won't end there and you know it."

Clay walked around the counter and leaned against it with arms crossed. His jaw set stubbornly. He was a determined man when he wanted something. And the blaze in his eyes told her what he wanted. "We're great in bed."

"I know," she said softly. It hurt her to think she'd never have that kind of passion again. That she may never know that same feeling of absolute satisfaction and completion. Her body may never sing with want and hum in the aftermath of lovemaking again. Mind-numbing sex hadn't been enough to hold their marriage together. And it certainly wasn't enough now. There was much more at stake than easing pent-up lust. Much, much more.

When Trish walked out on Clay, secretly she'd wanted an assurance that she was the right choice for him, that his love for her hadn't died with all the bickering and arguing. But that assurance never came. His motivation was clear: he was through with her. He wanted to move on.

She'd held the sum total of her marriage, the divorce papers, in her shaky hands that day and broken down, crying her eyes out. Her heart shattered and her stomach in turmoil, she hadn't eaten for days after. It was no surprise that she'd gotten sick and missed an entire week of work. Once she'd finally pulled herself together and gone back to the office, she'd become a different person—a person who knew she'd been right all along not to rely on Clay or anyone else for her happiness.

It was like seeing those empty seats in the school auditorium when she'd walked on stage, her parents the only ones MIA from their child's performance.

"While I'm here, I'm going to focus on the fundraiser for Penny's Song. I won't have a lot of time," she said, lifting her eyes to his, "for anything else."

Dubious, he cocked his head to one side and his eyes lit like sparks on the Fourth of July. "Count on me to change your mind."

Trish stood there rooted to the spot, unable to say a word. *Unfinished pleasure,* he'd called it.

Even as Clay came closer to kiss her forehead and say goodbye, she stood with shoulders stiff and prayed she hadn't made a giant, dumbass mistake.

By unwittingly posing a challenge to Clay.

It was the one thing her husband never passed up.

Five

With cattle in the distance and puffy white clouds gracing the sky, Trish parked the Volvo near the entrance to Penny's Song. She set Meggie in the Cadillac of strollers and headed over to the corrals to show her the horses.

Trish had grown up in Nashville, a city full of country music and honky-tonks, of crowded streets and great shopping. She wasn't an expert on horses, cattle or ranches, which came as a shock to those who didn't truly know her. Even though she'd made her home at Worth Ranch for a short while, she'd never really felt like she'd fit in here, so seeing the little ranch come to life was as much a treat for her as it was for the children here.

Today she would take everything in from her own perspective and lend a hand.

A girl came running out of the barn when she spotted them. "Hi!"

"Hello, Wendy." Trish smiled at the child she remembered from the other day.

"I just finished mucking out a stall." Wendy pinched her nose and made a freckled face frown with enough drama to win an acting award. "It's really stinky in there."

Amused, Trish laughed. "I bet it is."

"But I earned tokens. And later today, I get to buy something at the general store. I've been saving up for Cuddles." Wendy's chest swelled with pride.

"What's a Cuddles?"

"A kitty. With tiger eyes."

"Oh, that sounds nice." Trish assumed the feline was a stuffed animal.

"After I get her, can I show the baby?" She lifted her chin to meet with Trish's eyes.

"Of course. Meggie would like that."

The little girl touched Meggie's hand and the baby cooed, giving her a small toothless smile. Wendy lingered for a moment and when lunch was called by the sounding of an iron triangle, she rose and headed to the saloon.

Trish spent the rest of the afternoon in the general store, spelling the college-aged boy named Preston, whose services were needed at the stables. Meggie cooperated by falling fast asleep in the parked stroller inside, behind the counter. Trish had become familiar with the items on display for purchase. They were quite a mix of old and new. Stuffed animals, board games and toys populated the shelves as well as wrapped candies in mason jars. There were DVD movies, all age-appropriate and a shelf full of books, both classics and newer collections. One wall of shelves held healthy snacks, apples and oranges in short crate barrels, along with crunchy granola bars and snack crackers.

The job was a breeze. When Meggie woke up, Trish fed her a bottle and held her in her arms, slowly walking the length of the store, showing the baby items that fascinated her. Five eager young customers had come in at different times, browsing the shelves, and were equally excited to see Meggie again. The baby had fun interacting with them. Trish noted how each one of the children, no matter the age, seemed to have a real appreciation for Penny's Song and their own role in making the ranch work.

Wendy came in last that day with a cheerful hello for Trish.

"Hello again, Wendy. You're here for Cuddles, right?"

Wendy nodded and walked over to the stuffed animals on the shelf, eyeing the white ball of fluff with two golden eyes. "I've saved up my tokens all week."

"She's very cute, but are you sure that's what you want?"

Wendy grinned wide, showing a gap in her mouth where two teeth were missing. "It's for my sister. She's five and she's been lonely for me."

Trish swallowed hard. Tears burned behind her eyes. She didn't have words and found herself speechless, stunned by the girl's selfless generosity. Wendy had been the ill one. She'd gone through an ordeal which would make any child greedy for a little comfort, yet she'd thought of giving her younger sister a gift from her hard-won earnings. "That's... very nice of you. I'm sure your sister will love it."

Wendy headed to the bunkhouse, vowing to sleep with Cuddles for the next few days, to keep her safe until she could give the kitty to her sister. Trish closed up shop shortly after, her heart brimming with warmth for all the Wendys in the world. Penny's Song was a worthwhile venture, a charity to be proud of, and Trish was glad she'd made the effort to come and bear witness to it.

Just as she was pushing Meggie in her stroller toward the car, she spotted Jackson Worth, Clay's brother, coming out of the barn deep in conversation with Suzy Johnson. The warm fuzzies she was feeling instantly turned cold. The sensation wrapped itself around her like a frigid sheet of ice.

The woman was laughing, her dark mane of hair bouncing on her shoulders as she moved alongside Trish's brother-in-law. Her cheery disposition annoyed Trish. It was something she'd have to reconcile for the next few weeks.

Suzy was doing a good thing by volunteering, but a little voice inside her head chose to ignore that rational thought. Suzy wasn't the root of her problems with Clay, but she'd been a catalyst and the last person she wanted to speak with at the moment.

Jackson caught sight of her and waved. Oh, man. Trish sucked in a breath and waved back. She wanted to be anywhere but here and wished the earth would do her a favor and swallow her up. More realistically, why hadn't she locked up the general store just five minutes earlier and avoided the whole situation? Her heart sank as the two strode over with purposeful strides, heading straight for her.

Trish kept her eyes trained on her stunningly handsome brother-in-law. Forcing a hint of a smile, she waited while they approached.

"Trisha Fontaine. I'd heard you were back at the ranch." Jackson gave her a bear hug, drawing her tight to his chest. She'd always liked Jackson and she hugged him back with genuine affection. In a smooth move, he set her away to size her up, his easy gaze roaming over her from top to bottom. "You're looking good, sis."

"Hi, Jackson." He was the only one she'd let get away with calling her Trisha. And he relished it. The man was ten times charming when he set his mind to it and many said he most resembled his legendary great-great-great-grandfather, Chance Worth, with his dark brooding eyes and seductive smile. "I've been here a few days. Where have you been?"

With a shrug, he sent her a stunner of a grin. "Getting into trouble."

She had to smile back at him. "No doubt."

Suzy stepped forward. "Hi, Trish."

"Hello, Suzy," she said warmly enough. She refused to feel inferior and let the woman get the best of her, despite the ease she had with the Worth men.

"I heard about your friend's death and I'm sorry for it." Suzy gave a pitying glance at Meggie in the stroller. "You taking the baby and raising her, it's very noble."

"Thank you. It's the right thing to do." She kept a civil tone. "Meggie's a true joy in my life. She's very sweet-natured."

Right on cue, Meggie let out an ear-piercing wail.

Trish did a mental eye roll.

Jackson's smile never wavered. "She's a beauty. With a healthy pair of lungs."

Suzy pointed at the baby, making an observation. "Healthy and *wet*. Looks like there's a leak."

And sure enough, Trish glanced down to see a wet spot underneath the baby, the stream of moisture fanning out onto the quilted padding lining the stroller. "Oh my goodness. Where did that come from?"

She bent to the baby, offering silent apologies and lifted her out of the stroller. Trish knew exactly where that had come from. She'd forgotten to change the diaper while she was working in the general store and now the baby was letting the whole world know.

Heat rushed up her cheeks immediately as she tried to soothe Meggie's cries with some quiet shushing and rocking. Meggie was having none of it. The only answer was to make a hasty escape and be done with it. "I'd better get going," she rushed out without sparing Suzy a glance. "I'll change her in the car. It's good seeing you two."

But Jackson wouldn't let her run off. He gripped her arm gently before she turned, coming to her rescue. "I'll get the stroller and help you load it into the car."

"Thanks." Out of the corner of her eye, she saw Suzy's brows knit together and a look of utter misgiving cross her features.

Geesh.

With the baby crying, the stroller destroyed and Nurse Suzy Johnson looking on, Trish had failed the most basic Motherhood for Dummies course, with a big fat *F.*

Trish pulled up to Tagg's house and parked the car, her nerves just about shot. She'd gotten over her initial humiliation today—though it felt like she'd been caught with her pants down—and managed to rationalize the entire event in her mind as a diaper malfunction. The diaper had been faulty with tabs that lost their sticking power and had leaked like a faucet. It was an accident that could have happened to even the most astute mother, she told herself even though she'd promised Meggie she'd do better in the future. She'd managed to wash the stains out of the stroller and blow dry the quilted padding until it looked as good as new. The material was made for accidents of the moist kind, it seemed. Trish was grateful for that.

I'm the one taking the baby steps.

She had to stop thinking like that, yet those dubious thoughts filtered in and made her doubt herself and her abilities time and again.

She got out of the car and opened the back passenger door. "We'll just drop off the cake and be off," she said to her chubby-cheeked baby.

Meggie turned to the sound of her voice with her eyes bright, filled with trust. A powerful jolt of love rushed through Trish's system. She couldn't believe how much she loved the little fourteen-pound bundle of mischief.

At one time, Trish wondered if she'd ever get to this point with Meggie. She recalled those first few days after

CHARLENE SANDS 87

Karin died. How difficult it had been, being the replacement mother, knowing Meggie sensed the difference and seemed out of sorts and hard to handle. Although she was familiar with Trish, she hadn't known her in the mothering role and her sharp instincts had taken hold. It had been weeks before she accepted her. Now the baby placed her full faith in her, seeming to forgive her mothering blunders.

She lifted Meggie in her arms, and after the day she had, decided not to press her luck by juggling the baby and the lemon chiffon cake in her arms. She'd ask for help from Tagg or Callie when she got to the front door.

She took a few steps toward the house, when a pickup truck pulled up and parked behind her car. Clay appeared, bounding out of the cab and as she blinked away her surprise, she did a mental eye roll.

She couldn't seem to catch a break today.

"Hey," he said, glancing at Meggie first with a soft flicker in his eyes. Then as he approached, his gaze flowed over Trish from top to bottom like warm, thick honey. It was a Worth trait, the ability to send molten-liquid looks to women. When Clay sent one her way—as if he was remembering every inch of her naked flesh—her nerves met with unwelcome tingles as if he'd physically stroked her.

"Hey, yourself."

"They didn't tell me you'd be here," he said. She wondered how he'd meant that. His expression was unreadable.

"I'm not. Here. I'm just stopping by for a second. I made Tagg and Callie a cake."

"Oh, yeah? What kind?"

"Lemon chiffon. Helen helped me. I screwed up the batter the first time."

Clay's grin spread his mouth wide. His bruises were still there, but Trish looked beyond them to his handsome face. "Helen? Oh, man, where is it?"

She pointed to the car.

"I'll bring it in," he said with boyish eagerness.

"That's not—" But then she caught herself. The sooner she could deliver the cake and thank the Worths, the sooner she could be on her way. "Thank you. Could you bring the book bag, too?"

"Sure thing."

Not only did he retrieve the items she'd asked for, he also slung the diaper bag over his shoulder. She should tell him that it wasn't necessary, she wouldn't be staying long enough to need it. But he'd caught her by surprise. He'd find out soon enough.

"It's nice that you visit your brother," she said, making small talk to fill the silence as they walked along the path to the front door.

"More like, I'm being hijacked. After the accident yesterday, Callie insisted on having me over for dinner. She wouldn't take no for an answer, and I'm not about to argue with a pregnant lady."

"You're feeling better today?"

She shouldn't have asked. She shouldn't care so much, but he was still her husband and a man she once loved very much.

His voice lowered in a sensual rasp meant for her ears only. "Yeah, you cured me last night, remember?"

A hot flush sped up her throat to singe her cheeks. "Clay."

His eyes smoldered as if he were reliving the memory of last night's lovemaking, and Trish fell into the trap of recollection. She couldn't suppress those memories either, not with Clay beside her. Breathing in his rugged scent and hearing the rich, sexy tone of his voice made her painfully aware of him as the man who'd taken her to heaven last night. She kept on walking, grateful Clay's hands were otherwise occupied. She wouldn't stand a chance if he touched her.

The baby squirmed against her body and Trish's focus

was brought back to reality. She put things in perspective as she shifted the baby onto her other arm and settled her into a more comfortable position. The distraction was appreciated and necessary.

Score one for Meggie.

When they reached the front door, Clay knocked. They stood there together, the three of them, Clay with the covered cake in his hands and Trish with the baby in her arms. To anyone who didn't know better, they would have looked like a true family of three. Trish squelched the idea quickly when the door opened.

Callie didn't seem surprised to see her. Instead, she offered a gracious welcome. "Come in, both of you. Trish, I'm glad you stopped by. You're staying for dinner, of course. I've made enough for an army."

"Oh, no," she said as Clay allowed her to enter the house first. "I couldn't impose. I made a cake, well, with some major help, and I hear it's Tagg's favorite."

Tagg appeared behind his wife and took interest in the cake holder Clay held. "You made lemon chiffon?"

It was as if Trish's stock went up, judging by the look of approval on his face. "Guilty as charged. It's a thank-you for lending me the baby equipment. I've been using everything." She wouldn't reveal how much Meggie had "used" the stroller today. Trish was going to replace it with a new one, when the time came to give the equipment back. "It was very generous of both of you."

"Happy to help out," Tagg said, and Callie agreed. "But I won't say you shouldn't have. I'd sell my soul for lemon chiffon."

"It's wonderful that you're here," Callie said. "And you have to stay. I have a hundred questions for you about babies." She glanced at Meggie and smiled, stroking the baby's soft cheek with her finger. "You have hands-on experience with this little one."

Callie spoke directly to the baby with the softest whisper. "You remember me, don't you?"

Meggie didn't react, she only watched Callie with interest.

Callie put a hand on her belly. "I can't wait."

Then Callie turned to Clay and shook her head. "You gave us a scare yesterday." She walked straight into his arms and hugged him the best she could. Between her growing belly and the things Clay held in his hand, it wasn't much of an embrace, but it was obvious that Callie and Clay had a good relationship.

"I'm fine," Clay offered mildly, as if she was making a big deal out of nothing.

Callie ushered them into the parlor and Clay handed Tagg the cake and Callie the book bag.

Trish explained, "I'm no expert on babies, but I brought you five books that I found very useful. I've highlighted the key points and made notes in the margins."

Callie peeked inside the bag, her eyes lighting up. "Wow, you sure did. These are great. I can't wait to start reading them, but I still want to pick your brain. Have a seat. Dinner will be on shortly." She hugged the books to her chest and walked into the kitchen.

It was a done deal. Trish couldn't back out now and disappoint her. She'd seem ungrateful.

"Thanks again for the cake," Tagg said with a grin. "My stomach's on high alert now. I've been craving lemon chiffon."

Trish sent up a silent prayer that her culinary skills wouldn't disappoint. "I hope it turned out okay."

"He'll have to fight me for seconds," Clay said with a crooked smile.

"Looks like you've already been in a fight." Tagg scoured over Clay's injuries with an assessing eye.

Clay rubbed the back of his neck and released a heavy sigh. "To be honest, it felt that way yesterday. But this morning, I woke up feeling great." Clay darted a quick glance her way and it was all she could do not to react. She willed her body to stay still. She kept her expression unreadable. It wasn't an easy task. She'd wring Clay's neck, adding to his injuries, if he made one mention of their night together.

But luckily, the conversation changed to the latest cattle prices and Clay's new car purchase. When Tagg exited the room to help Callie in the kitchen, Trish pulled a small blanket and soft foam baby book out of the diaper bag and put Meggie down on the floor.

"I hear you bumped into Jackson today at Penny's Song," Clay said.

Trish lowered herself to the carpet and sat in a tailor position with legs crossed to face Meggie. She gazed up at him. He leaned forward on the sofa, arms braced on his knees. "It was good to see him. Same old Jackson."

"Yeah, he doesn't change."

"News travels fast," she said. "Did he...did he tell you about the baby-stroller fiasco?"

Clay's lack of reaction gave her pause. He didn't answer. He said nothing at all, and then it dawned on her. It wasn't Jackson, but Suzy who'd relayed the information about their meeting.

Trish let that sink in. Suzy had a direct pipeline to Clay and seemed to be in touch with him in one way or another every day. No doubt now, Clay had been informed about their meeting from Suzy's perspective. "Never mind," she said, shrugging it off. She wasn't going to let Suzy Johnson ruin her evening. "It isn't important."

Clay dropped down onto the floor. His musky scent filled

her nostrils as he sat in the same manner beside her and picked up the baby book. "No, it's not important."

He opened the book and pressed his finger to a chicken's mouth on the first page. The book clucked and Meggie bounced with excitement, waving her arms and lifting in a little jump. She cackled her approval and Clay grinned. "So easy to make some women happy."

Stunned at his train of thought, Trish's mouth gaped open.

Clay leaned over and kissed it closed. His lips were warm and his touch was gentle. Trish was caught entirely off guard by the shocking beauty of this stolen moment. With Meggie looking on and his family in the other room, Trish couldn't give way to protest even if the notion crossed her mind. Which it did not. Instead, she enjoyed the interlude and the delicious taste of him. When he broke off the kiss and pulled back, he gazed into her eyes with a mix of amusement and heat.

"I've never been *some women*," Trish said softly.

Clay whispered near her ear, his voice a rasp of desire. "I know."

Callie's voice came from just outside the parlor door. "Dinner is ready."

Trish pulled away from Clay, guilt washing over her. She felt like a schoolgirl being caught with a boy under the bleachers. But when she peered at Callie in the doorway, she didn't seem to notice.

Clay bounded up. "I'm starving."

He reached down and lent her a hand up. Trish took his outstretched hand and got to her feet, then straightened, but before she could reach for Meggie, Clay was there, scooping her up into his arms. "Ready?" he asked, the picture of innocence, holding the baby.

Meggie seemed thoroughly enthralled with Clay. All of

Trish's good intentions to prevent the baby from bonding with him seemed to be falling by the wayside.

Tonight especially, Trish was helpless to stop it.

After dinner, the men went to the stables to check out Tagg's stallions while Callie and Trish stayed at the dining table. Trish enlightened Callie with the small bit of knowledge she had about motherhood and babies. But Callie had assured her that all of her insight was valued. She hadn't asked hard questions, but rather tapped into her experience with baby bottles, bath time, sleep issues and immunizations. All things Trish had already gone through with Meggie.

"She's due for another round of immunizations when we get back home," Trish said. "I keep a running record in a file to make sure I don't miss anything."

"That's good to know...but—" Callie didn't finish her thought. Her lips pursed in hesitation. She was holding something back.

"You look puzzled," Trish said.

Callie shook her head. "It's just...well. Never mind. It's none of my business."

Trish sent Callie a glance, thinking better of bringing up the subject, but compelled to do so anyway. "You're wondering about my relationship with Clay."

Her return to Red Ridge was probably the talk of the town, so Callie's question wasn't a surprise.

"You said you were going home, but I couldn't help notice the way you look at Clay."

Trish understood immediately and the explanation fell easily from her lips. "You're married to a Worth. You know the drill. They are charming when they want to be and very easy on the eye. But it's complicated with me and Clay."

"Tagg and I had similar issues. We were able to resolve them."

Trish glanced at the hand Callie laid over her growing belly. The baby bump meant new life grew there, a Worth child. It was monumental. "You have a baby coming. Babies can bring a couple together. Or they can tear them apart. That is, if one is ready and the other isn't."

"But now you have Meggie."

"Yes, but she isn't Clay's." She added softly, "The baby isn't a bargaining chip."

"Oh, I didn't mean that—"

Trish laid her hand over Callie's and squeezed gently. "I know you didn't. It's just that what went wrong with my marriage hasn't got anything to do with Meggie. I'm here for a short time. I will go back to Nashville and resume my life there. Anything between Clay and me would be pointless and well, frankly, too hard to deal with. I've already had my heart broken once."

"Trish, I'm so sorry. I guess I figured if Tagg and I could work out our problems, then maybe you and Clay could, too. Selfish of me to hope for that. I'd love to have a sister-in-law on the ranch. I'd love it if we became close friends. And Meggie," Callie said with true affection, "would be part of the family."

A nice dream in a perfect world.

Trish reassured her. "We'll always be your friends."

Callie nodded as if she understood completely, but then she lowered her voice. "You know how you look at Clay? Well, he looks at you the same way." Callie's lips formed a brilliant smile. "Sorry, but I just had to say it. And now I'll shut up."

Trish's eyes widened and she joined Callie in a smile, but with a serious shake of her head.

When the men came back in, Callie served dessert. The lemon chiffon cake turned out better than Trish could have hoped. Tagg and Clay ate two big slices with compliments to the chef. Once dessert was finished, Trish was ready to get Meggie and *herself* off to bed. It had been a long eventful day and all things considered, not a bad one after all. She really enjoyed getting to know Callie and spending time with Tagg. As long as she remembered why she'd come to Worth Ranch, she'd do fine.

Holding the baby in one arm, she reached over with the other arm to give Callie and Tagg a hug. "Thanks for a delicious meal and good company."

"I should be thanking you for letting me pick your brain," Callie said. "Just seeing Meggie in action makes me anxious for our little one to arrive."

"Me, too." Tagg kissed Callie on the cheek and then turned his megawatt smile on Trish. "Will you give Callie the recipe for that cake?"

"I sure will."

Callie bumped Tagg's side with a deliberate and gentle swing of her hips that he didn't seem to mind at all. "He's always thinking of his stomach."

An arm came around to pull Callie in. "I'm always thinking of *your* stomach, although mine is humming a happy tune right now."

Trish looked on smiling. "Well, I'd better get the baby to bed."

"I'll walk you out," Clay said, resolute, gathering up the diaper bag. There was no point in refusing, Clay was already nearing the door. His determined look had Trish feeling a little wary. She waited as he thanked his sister-in-law for the dinner, then he shook his brother's hand.

Outside, spring breezes whipped Trish's hair away from her face. Tagg's house sat at a higher elevation than the main house along the base of the mountain where the air was fresher and crisper. A moonlit stream interrupted the stark darkness as they ambled toward the cars together, Meggie wiggling in her arms. She rubbed her eyes with balled fists.

"She looks tired," Clay noted.

"She is. She had a busy day." On a sigh, Trish confessed. "We both did."

Clay spoke in a low voice. "I need to talk to you."

"We need to discuss the divorce. We'll reschedule."

"Not about that." The muscles in his jaw flinched. "It's about the fundraiser."

By then, they'd reached her car and Clay carefully took Meggie out of her arms while she fished for her keys. She opened the door wide and turned in time to see Meggie's head come to rest against Clay's chest. Trish heard his breath catch as Meggie curled her chubby body right into his. He splayed his hand over her back securing her position, tucking her head under his chin. Stroking her hair with a light touch, he stood there for a moment simply holding her.

Meggie was becoming more and more familiar with Clay. She responded to his gentle manner and confidence with un-wavering trust the way a daughter would her father. It was what Trish most feared. She didn't want them to bond. She didn't want Meggie to feel any loss when they left Arizona. Heaviness centered in Trish's chest and a twinge of what could have been flashed before her eyes, watching the two of them together.

Clay seemed to read her thoughts and the moment was wrought with unspoken regret. "I'll put her in now," he said finally.

Trish nodded with a whispered, "She'll probably be out like a light soon."

Clay made sure Meggie was safely fastened in the car seat and then rose to meet her gaze. "We've got a dinner appoint-ment tomorrow night with the manager at the Ridgecrest Hotel. The place is new, on the outskirts of town and as you know, they'd volunteered their main room and offered a big discount on catering services for the gala."

Trish blinked at the way Clay casually made that announcement. "I'm still trying to get past the 'we' part. Why did you make an appointment without consulting me first?"

On a casual shrug, Clay answered, "It was a last-minute thing. There are loose ends that need tying up. The manager prattled on about the gala's theme and decorations. I don't know a darn thing about that stuff."

That much was true. Clay knew how to rope a steer, soothe a ruffled employee's nerves and keep his empire running smoothly, but he had no skill in setting up an event like this. That was her department. She could organize a fundraiser like this with one hand tied behind her back. "But can't we meet with him during the day?"

"He was adamant about tomorrow night."

Trish frowned. "It's just…Meggie. She goes to bed, well, at this time of night. You see how tired she is now. She'll be cranky and I won't be able to focus on business."

"Then we'll bring Helen along. She can watch her for an hour or two."

Trish mulled that over. "What time is the appointment?"

"Eight o'clock."

Clay's solution was viable. Trish might not have been so easily persuaded if she hadn't had second thoughts about how the fundraiser should be handled. Working at Penny's Song today brought a clearer understanding of their mission. She'd seen the facility with a new pair of eyes and ears, witnessing the interactions between the volunteers and children. She would have to discuss this with Clay first, but Trish knew a better way to raise money for the charity than a luxurious gala set in a hotel. She knew what would tug at people's heartstrings as well as their purse strings.

"Okay, then." With a snap of her head, she'd made her decision. "If it needs doing, we'll get it done."

Clay's lips curved up and a devastating smile reached his dark eyes.

"Why are you grinning like a silly fool?"

He didn't look like a silly fool—he looked one-hundred-percent male and gorgeous to boot. Wicked thoughts crowded her mind.

"You're sexy when you're all business."

"I...am?" Floored, she leaned heavily against the opened car door. This reminded her of when they were first dating. Clay would undress her with his eyes, explaining how her sharp wit turned him on. Whenever she'd talked business with him in all seriousness, he'd find a way to strip her of her acumen and her clothes.

"Yeah, you are." His eyes darkened to black pools and the smile that wasn't silly at all, shifted to something dangerous. He took a predatory step toward her and Trish wasn't strong enough to move away. What could he possibly do in front of his brother's house?

A lot, she found out soon enough.

He tipped her chin up with his thumb and brought his face close, so close that she could see the ink-black rim of his irises, so close that the seductive gleam in his eyes set her heart racing, so close that his warm breath fanned her cheeks. He dipped his head. Their eyes met. He made her wait. Then he kissed her, with the slightest teasing touch of his mouth.

That first brushing of their lips was tender and warm and just what she'd needed after a long, tiring day. When it came to matters of the flesh, Clay had a sense of when to go hot and when to simmer.

The simmering could be just as deadly.

His hand went to her cheek and he stroked her with the backside of his fingertips. Her body inched closer, absorbing the comfort and the heady sensation of being touched with such care. His lips came over hers again with the same degree of tenderness and feathery ripples of desire floated through her body. There was no demand, no pursuit of control in his kiss. Trish was defenseless against this tactic. She fell further and further, deriving immense pleasure from the scent of musk and man surrounding her. He moved his lips ever so slightly on hers with a mastery that elicited a thrill from the depths of her belly. Inches separated them and Trish found herself being pulled by a subtle force that belied her own stubborn resistance.

Clay on the other hand, was controlled and *sweet,* if she could describe such a rugged man that way.

She was tempted to fit herself to him, to feel the strong planes of his body and wrap herself into the comfort of his muscular arms. She wanted to be pressed skin to skin with him, and that feeling wouldn't go away.

His hand traveled down the hollow beneath her chin to her throat. She pulsed there and in every other erogenous zone she possessed, waiting, wanting. His index finger touched where she throbbed frantically and the world stopped as he took a deep inhalation of breath.

Turmoil sped through her system. She *wanted* him. But other forces held her in check, forces he could easily overturn. But he made no such demands of her. He only kissed her gently one last time.

Then he pulled away.

She witnessed the exact moment of his mental retreat, the sizzling gleam in his beautiful eyes slowly diffusing.

"Get some sleep," he said. "I'll see you tomorrow."

The lump in her throat she swallowed past was pride. She could only nod and watch him saunter away. He opened the door to his truck and waited until she got in the car and started it up, before his engine roared to life.

Trish drove home with Clay's headlights reflecting in her rearview mirror.

When she turned onto her drive, his truck kept going, moving down the road to the main house.

"That was close, baby," she whispered, her heart in her throat.

She didn't understand the tears that stung behind her eyes.

Or maybe she did, and that was why her heart ached so badly with disappointment.

Six

Clay opened the door to his new Mercedes sedan gesturing with a sweep of his hand for Trish to get in. Petal sleeves fell from her shoulders in a flow of soft pink as her summery dress nudged at her knees. Matching heels brought her up several inches to meet his eyes, and the whole package as Trish stood there beside him put his luxurious car to shame. Damn, but his wife cleaned up nicely. He'd done the same, trading in his ranch attire for dark trousers and a white silver-studded shirt. He wore a black Stetson and polished boots.

Trish didn't seem to notice him or the car.

Turning, she glanced at the front door one last time, nibbling on her ruby glossed lips. Her brows gathered together like storm clouds.

"Go on and enjoy your evening," Helen called from the doorway. "The baby will be fine."

Trish took a swallow. If she were going to her own execution she couldn't have looked more forlorn. She cast Helen a sick smile and then spun slowly around.

"You ready?" he asked.

Her head bobbed absentmindedly. "I think so."

Clay grinned. "Then jump in."

Trish wasn't doing any jumping tonight. Every move was slow and deliberate. "Oh, okay."

He took her sweater and purse from her hands and helped her into the front seat. She cast a longing look at the front door. Helen gave a final wave of encouragement and disappeared inside the house.

Once he was behind the wheel, he turned to her. "Well, what do you think?"

"What do I think about what?" She looked at him, puzzled.

Distracting her wasn't easy. "My new ride."

"Oh." She took in the buttery almond leather seats and the dashboard that sported more buttons than a jet's cockpit. "It's nice. Different than what you usually drive." Then she glanced around really taking a good look. She swiveled her head to the back. "It's roomy. Are you out of the sports car phase?"

"At my age, one would hope." When he'd bought the car, it was with family in mind. This time around speed and sleekness hadn't been his first priority. He wanted something larger, sturdier and one that would hold a car seat or two. Wasn't a far stretch to say that the sooner he filled up those car seats, the better. He wasn't getting any younger. Men had mental biological clocks…and his was ticking like crazy.

"Thirty-six isn't exactly old. I don't see any mold growing off your chest, uh, you know what I mean."

He smiled, amused at her reference. "Thirty-seven. I had a birthday a few months back."

Chagrined, Trish only smiled and wished him a belated birthday. Then she became very quiet, her mind a million miles away. She was worried about Meggie. Leaving her with Helen hadn't been in the plans, but the baby had fallen asleep earlier than expected. Clay and Helen had a hard time convincing Trish to leave her asleep in her crib rather than disrupt her sleep. She'd hated doing it, but finally she'd agreed. It was obvious Trish couldn't keep her mind on anything else.

"She's fine," he said, turning slightly. With one eye on the road and one eye on her, Clay tried to reassure her.

Her lips formed a perfect pout. That look had once made Clay want to give her the world. "She's never been without me."

"You said yourself, she's a good sleeper."

"What if she wakes up and I'm not there?"

"Helen is a pro with kids. She'll rock her back to sleep."

"I know she's good with children," Trish said. "She promised to call me in an hour."

"So see, honey, if there's a problem, she'll let you know. But there won't be."

Clay was sure of it. Trish was overprotective when it came to Meggie, but in the short time she'd been here, for all her concerns, fears and misgivings to the contrary, Trish was turning out to be a wonderful mother. The doubtful look on her face and concern in her eyes tugged at something elemental and deep in his heart. It was hard to be angry with someone who cared so much, who tried so hard. She got an A for effort. Clay had known from the start it would be this way. The family that they could have had together would have been provided for, cherished and nurtured in the best possible way. Trish hadn't trusted in that.

But Clay had always known. It had been a bone of contention in their marriage and something he couldn't quite forget. Anger and impatience had destroyed his love for her and made him look to another woman for the things he wanted in

life. By the time Trish had gotten here, he was on the precipice with Suzy Johnson, but hadn't yet taken the plunge.

"I hope you're right," she uttered softly.

She nibbled on her lower lip again and uncertainty marred
her pretty face. A primal instinct took hold in his gut. Protective feelings surfaced that surprised him in their intensity. With a full-out cocky grin, Clay caught her attention.
"I always am."

Her lips curved up, amusement reaching her eyes, and she
shook her head at his nonsense. Mission accomplished, he
thought and the hell of it was, his own mood elevated with
the glimmer of Trish's smile.

They reached the Ridgecrest Resort Hotel in twenty minutes and met with Bruce Williams, the manager. He gave
them a brief overview of the resort's amenities and took them
on a tour of the grounds. It was an impressive piece of land,
with waterfall pools, spas and golf greens that rivaled PGA
championship courses.

On the way to the meeting rooms, Helen called to reassure them Meggie was still sleeping peacefully. Trish visibly sighed with relief. Her shoulders relaxed and contrary to
her calmer demeanor went straight into business mode. Her
sharp eyes took everything in. Clay saw her mind working,
clicking away, calculating and weighing options.

They reached the largest of the meeting rooms, a ball-
room adorned by eye-catching crystal chandeliers, a cur-
tained stage and polished dance floors suitable for waltzes or
the two-step. Clay liked the looks of the place. He blew out a
low whistle, imagining contributors dining here and opening
their wallets for a good cause. Trish looked on, effortlessly
giving polite smiles to Mr. Williams, but Clay's sixth sense
told him something was up with her.

"And if you'll allow me, I'll show you to our dining room,
where you may sample from a variety of meals we offer."

Williams, a middle-aged man with thin sandy hair and a perpetual smile, showed them to their table that overlooked the first tee of the golf course and the stunning Red Ridge Mountains beyond. The minute they sat down, Williams was called away and begged their apologies.

"Please, enjoy the meal. I'll return as soon as I can to answer your questions," he said.

Clay turned to Trish once he was gone. He'd always trusted her opinion on business matters. "What do you think?"

She paused a long moment, without saying a word. Clay couldn't gauge her reaction. Eyes wary now and narrowed on her, he said, "We're lucky they volunteered the use of the room. Red Ridge Inn can't accommodate nearly as many folks."

Trish's gaze swept over the hotel dining room one more time and then she leaned forward across the table. On her cue, he did the same. Inches separated them as they stared at each other, their breaths mingling.

She lowered her voice. "It's not right, Clay. I wanted to see this place to give it my full consideration. I've seen enough."

Her hair moved softly onto her face as she shook her head. Blond streaks caught the glow of light and Clay's mind wandered, for a second, thinking how he wanted this night to end. With Trish beside him in bed. "Okay," he said, unsure of where she was going with this. "What do you have in mind?"

Trish looked at him with new regard as he gave her a chance to explain. He wouldn't overreact. She'd always led him on the right path in business. That hadn't been the root of their trouble at all.

"It's tricky. We don't have much time. If I was here to begin with, I would have known." Again, she moved her head as if shaking off the thought. "We can't have the fundraiser here. It should be held at Penny's Song. It has to be, Clay."

He absorbed that with a nod. "I'm listening."

"I've seen Penny's Song in action. I've met the kids and seen the joy on their faces. The relationship they have with 〜 volunteers and each other is gratifying. In only a few days, I've come to know how very important the little ranch is to everyone involved. You can't walk away from a day at Penny's Song without feeling good. Benefactors and donors won't see that here. They won't get that from a slide show set to music. They need to walk the same ground as the kids. Get the lay of the land. See the bunkhouse, the general store and the saloon. We can still have a gala with catered food, china-set tables and entertainment. We can do it all and in the process get more bang for our buck if we do it at Penny's Song."

Clay envisioned the gala from Trish's point of view and he was floored. She hit the nail on the head and it was so dang obvious now that he should have thought of it himself. If Trish had been here during construction, he was sure they would have come to this conclusion together. "Damn, you're right. But it's short notice and what about Williams? He's expecting us to—"

"The only thing Mr. Williams will lose out on is volunteering his room. We'll still use the hotel's catering services. And we'll make darn sure that his resort is the place our out-of-town guests will stay when they come to Red Ridge. Trust me, Clay. This is going to work. I'll make phone calls tomorrow and make sure everyone attending knows the location has changed. As for the Red Ridge residents, those who already aren't volunteering will get a chance to see Penny's Song from our perspective. The goodwill the gala produces in the community will go a long way."

"Okay," Clay said, embracing the idea. "We'll get out the word and make the necessary changes." When Bruce Williams walked back into the dining room with his ever-present smile, Clay spared him a glance, then turned to Trish. "But who's going to break the news to the manager?"

Trish was a good sport. She handled Williams with kid gloves and even had him thanking her for the opportunity to be a part of Penny's Song's gala when all was said and done. Clay had to admire Trish in action. She was good at her job and he had no doubt that she'd make the fundraiser a huge success.

Dinner was served and they discussed the new plans over the meal. The whole time Trish was talking Clay listened, but it was the lilting tone of her voice, the low rasp at times and then the excited rise when something new occurred to her, that kept his rapt attention. She was beautiful in the soft glimmer of candlelight, and when Helen called, interrupting their meal to give Trish peace of mind, Clay saw his chance for a few stolen moments alone with her later.

They sipped wine, and after the meal, Clay ordered espresso and Raspberry Decadence from the dessert menu.

"Oh…this shouldn't be legal," she whispered, taking a bite and closing her eyes. The five-layer chocolate cake oozed with a filling of warm fudge drizzled with tart raspberry sauce. Her oohs and aahs continued, coming deep from her throat. The noises were sexy as hell. He didn't know how much more he could take. He sipped coffee watching her while every nerve jumped against his skin.

When she realized he hadn't touched his cake, her eyes fluttered and an adorable pout formed on her lips. "You're not having some?"

"Trust me, honey," he said, scraping the words out, "I'm getting *some*."

Her mouth pursed in puzzlement and Clay lifted just enough to lean over the table and tongued a dollop of raspberry sauce from the corner of her mouth. His move elicited a soft little "oh" from her lips and Clay's willpower crashed and burned. He moved his mouth half an inch and met with her ready lips. The kiss was hot but swift, *not nearly enough*. He leaned back in his seat, staring at Trish and the look on her face sent a blast of heat to his groin. Rising from the table, he offered her a hand up. "Let's get out of here."

Trish's momentary surprise quickly faded into something Clay could only deem as surrender when she took his hand. He led her outside.

No words were spoken as he strode to the back of a pool house, far away from the hotel's activities. The only sound he heard was the quiet hum of water falling from a cluster formation of rocks over the tropical pool. Clay leaned against the wall and tugged her to him, the extent of his desire revealed as their hips meshed. "You've got me horny as a teenager." He growled into her hair and pushed her petal sleeve down to nibble on her shoulder.

"I don't know what I did." Her whisper flowed over him, breathless.

Not much, he admitted. She never had to do too much to turn him on. And now that he'd had a taste of her again, he wanted more. "The way you took that cake into your mouth and moaned. Made me wish it was me."

Clay didn't give her a chance to respond. He brought his mouth over hers in an urgent melding of lips that defied reluctance on her part. He kissed her senseless, slanting his mouth over hers, making her grind out those little sounds, this time, for him.

Her hair slid through his fingers and he yanked gently, bringing her face slightly back to expose the slender slope of her neck. So beautiful. He kissed her with his tongue stroking a line over her soft skin. She smelled erotic in her innocent citrus scent. Next, he moved farther down to the plump ridge of her breasts. He held her firm with one hand to her hair, while the other thumbed her nipple through the silky fabric of her dress. The sensitive nipple responded to his touch immediately and he toyed with her until she pleaded for more. He replaced his thumb with his mouth giving her what she wanted. What *he* wanted. Trish gasped deep in her throat. His heartbeats sped out of control, her sounds sinful with raw need. He suckled her through the material, asking for more than decorum of place and time allowed. Yet, he'd grab whatever stolen minutes he could have with her, his common sense shattered.

She arched her back, allowing him more access and he stroked one breast with a heavy hand, kneading her through the protection of her clothes as he continued his assault on her other side with his mouth.

"Clay, pleeeeze." Her desperate plea tore through her throat.

"Hang on, honey." His body ached for release, yet Trish's needs came first. He'd brought her to this point. He would satisfy her, right here, right now.

He spun her around. Her rear end fit snugly against his erection and it pulsed with new life, but Clay held back. He couldn't take her here on the hotel grounds.

A little voice in his head begged to know *why not?*

"Clay." She squirmed against him.

His hand slipped under her dress. Her thigh filled his palm and he moved up slowly, relishing the feel of soft skin against his rough hand. She squirmed even more, aching, waiting with an intake of breath. Clay couldn't torment her, she needed him and as much as he wanted to bed her in the traditional way, she wasn't going home tonight unsatisfied.

He found her center. "Ah, man." She was wet and he knew this would be quick. Her passion made him ache in ways he couldn't begin to name.

He pushed aside her panties and stroked his finger over her core. She shuddered in his arms. "I know," he murmured against her ear.

"Are we really doing this?" Her softly spoken words sounded distant and incredulous as she leaned her head back.

Clay's answer was to slip his finger inside her. She trembled. And as he moved, she moved. They found a rhythm together that brought her higher and higher. He'd been right. Her climax came fast. Short and damn sweet as she uttered his name like a prayer. Her tremors made him break out in a sweat. He brought her to completion with one hand covering her mouth to keep her noisy gasps from echoing off the surrounding trees.

Clay kissed the back of her neck, holding her steady, letting her come down at her own speed. When she did, she turned slowly, her beautiful blue eyes glowing under a paltry beam of moonlight. "I've never been a selfish lover."

She set her hand on his belt buckle, her fingers splayed over his stirring erection. His need grew with every passing second. "Don't start something you can't finish," he warned with a growl of desire.

Drawing her lower lip inside her mouth, she blinked and hesitated. "Tell me this is only about sex."

Clay could tell her that. She needed to know it was a pre-divorce fling and nothing more. He hadn't forgiven her. She hadn't forgiven him. Maybe that's all it was and he was okay with that right now. "It's only about sex."

She unhooked his belt.

"Hey, you kids come outta there right now!" a gravelly voice commanded. "This is hotel security."

Clay met with Trish's wide, stunned eyes. She gasped and put herself back together with lightning speed.

"Come out, where I can see you." The beam of a flashlight darted in front of them. Clay heard footsteps approach.

He took Trish's hand and pulled her into the light with him. "It's okay, officer. I was just showing my wife the *sights*."

An elderly man in a blue uniform and hat appeared. His stern expression changed instantly when he saw them, and he relaxed his stance. Scratching his head and sighing deep, the guard asked, "What the heck kind of sights are you showing her this late at night?"

Clay kept his tone serious. "You'd be surprised."

The man shook his head as if the notion was ridiculous. "Thought you were kids doing what they shouldn't. You folks registered at the resort?"

"No, sir," Clay said earnestly. "We had business with Bruce Williams, the manager."

"That so?" he asked, still a little skeptical. Then his aging eyes sparked with recognition. It was the "look" Clay had come to know from days of being in the limelight. "Hey, aren't you that singer?"

"Yes, sir, I am."

"Clayton Worth, right?"

Clay nodded.

"You folks live around here." It was a statement of fact.

"Not far from here."

"Okay, well, then. You go on. I've got a maple bar and cup of coffee waiting on me back at the guard shack."

"Sure thing." Clay squeezed Trish's hand tighter and they walked toward the hotel with heads held high. As soon as the guard was out of view, they took off at a run heading toward the car, Trish keeping pace with him. When they reached the parking lot, Clay clicked open both doors and they jumped inside the car breathing heavily from their jaunt. With chests heaving, they turned to each other and the second their eyes met, they broke out laughing.

* * *

"Bet you'd never thought we'd almost get hauled to the slammer tonight," Clay said, amusement gleaming in his dark eyes. He leaned casually against her front door, brows arched devilishly.

She stood facing him and gave a nod. "It was a night for the books."

His eyes narrowed in concentration as he lifted a lock of her hair and studied it. "Yeah, it was."

She swallowed back the invitation on her lips. The evening didn't have to end. He was waiting for her to say so and oh, how she wanted to. They could have another mind-blowing night together.

"It's late. There's a lot of work to do tomorrow," she said finally, chickening out. Sometimes, Trish wished she could go for broke, damn the consequences and not be so rational in her thinking. Why couldn't she just invite him in for a wild time on the Trish Fontaine express and be done with it?

Because that's not you, that insipid voice in her head answered back.

Think of Meggie, she cautioned. She needs stability in her life now. In a quiet voice she said, "I should let Helen get home. It was nice of her to—"

Clay took her into his arms and kissed her. It was less urgent than before, less erotic. Savoring her mouth, he lingered on her lips and it was pure heaven to have him touch her this way. His lips felt familiar and oddly safe, as he demanded nothing from her. The kiss soothed her and brought a measure of peace to her heart and she kissed him back, relishing his giving lips and the warmth they brought with them.

Trish's heart tripped over itself. Something more than sex was happening here, at least on her part, and it scared her silly. She was ready to back away, denying them another soft and warm exchange of kisses, but then Clay surprised her by breaking their connection first.

He stepped back and searched her eyes, holding her captive for a long moment. She didn't know what to think now or how to feel, she just stared back at him.

"Tell Helen I'll give her a ride home," he said. "I'll be in the car waiting."

Trish opened her mouth to say something, but Clay had already turned away. She watched him walk to his car and get in.

"Oh, wow," she whispered into thin air.

The entire evening flashed before her eyes in a blur. She was dazed and confused. She opened the door and walked inside as if on autopilot, putting one foot in front of the other, her stomach tied in knots, her brain crowded with overwhelming thoughts. She tried to make sense of what was happening between her and her estranged soon-to-be ex-husband and nothing jumped out with clarity. Not one darn thing.

Helen approached her in the entry, taking in her appearance and most likely, the sated look on her face. "Clayton showed you a good time."

"Helen!"

Was it that apparent? Scorching heat rose up Trish's neck.

Helen giggled with youthful glee. Her entire face brightened and Trish felt the need to set her straight.

"He did not. I mean, it's not like that," she explained. "It's nothing. We talked business most of the time."

"Talking business usually doesn't muss your hair like you just woke up or put a dreamy look on your face and make an earring disappear."

Trish grabbed both her ears. One of her chandelier earrings was missing. "Oh! That was one of my favorites." Images popped into her head of how she could have lost it. Was it when Clay pulled her up against the pool-house wall and made love to her, shattering her body into a hundred pieces? Or maybe it was when he grabbed her hand and they took off running from the security guard. She couldn't contain the smile that dug into her cheeks.

Helen sent her an I-told-you-so look.

A change of subject was necessary. "How's Meggie?"

"Sleeping like an angel. She woke up once for a bottle. Drank a few ounces, then she was out again."

"I'm glad she was no trouble." She walked past Helen, toward the bedroom, eager to see the baby, and the older woman followed her into the room. Trish slowed as she approached the crib, putting both hands on the rim. Soft rays glowing from a Princess Cinderella night-light illuminated Meggie's sweet-cheeked slumber. With Helen beside her, they watched the baby's chest move up and down in peaceful breaths.

"She's precious to me," Trish whispered, feeling unmatched love in her heart. She wanted to protect Meggie from anything that could harm her. She wanted to ensure her a happy, fulfilling life. The baby deserved as much.

"Thank you for staying and watching her tonight. She was better off here. I knew she was in good hands."

"Anytime. I don't mind watching her if there's a need."

"I appreciate that." They reached the parlor where Helen picked up her handbag and sweater. "Oh, I almost forgot. You got a call from someone named John Stevenson." Helen walked over to the end table and picked up a note by the phone. "He couldn't reach you by your cell phone. Your assistant, Jodi, gave him this number. Here," she said, "I wrote down what he said." She handed her the note.

Trish's brows knitted together. She took a cursory glance at the note before lifting her gaze back to Helen. "Clay's waiting for you outside in the car. He'll drive you home."

"Oh dear, I didn't realize he was waiting on me. He didn't want to come in?"

"I didn't invite him in, Helen." She shook her head regretfully. There was no sense mincing words and at least now, Helen wouldn't get the wrong idea about the two of them. Quick pre-divorce flings did not heal a broken marriage.

Trish walked her out, and she felt an overwhelming urge to embrace Helen and thank her for her help. Helen hugged her back with a tight squeeze. The warmth in the older woman's eyes brought Trish immense happiness as they said goodbye.

Once back inside, Trish stared at the note from a Realtor in Nashville. The message read: "The house you wanted is back on the market. The seller is anxious. Are you still interested?"

The house was a little four-bedroom cottage on the outskirts of Nashville in a great school district. It had a big backyard with green grassy areas and a playhouse that the seller would leave, if the buyer wanted it. It was a picture-perfect house for a family. Even before Meggie had come into her life, Trish had loved that house. She'd driven by it every day on her way to the office. Now she had a chance to make that house a home for her small family.

Her mind spinning, Trish couldn't make the decision tonight. She had Clay on the brain and a dozen other things to sort out in her mind. "Tomorrow, or the next day," she muttered, convincing herself she'd have a clearer mind after a good night's sleep.

The morning came too fast. Meggie had woken up at 2:00 a.m. and heaven love her, wanted to be entertained before falling back to sleep. At six, Trish dragged herself out of bed to rise with the sun so that she could get some work done on Penny's Song before Meggie woke up again.

Groggy, but working efficiently under a deadline, Trish

made her plan for switching over the entire fundraiser to the little ranch. She put it all down on paper, designing the night's activities and how she would go about wowing the contributors in a much more understated way. She'd always believed in the soft sell.

By noon, Trish had commissioned for flyers to be spread around town and had even booked a spot on the local news for an interview. She'd make calls to benefactors in the next few days and in the upcoming weeks she'd pull out all the stops and work on the details, but for now the wheels were set in motion for the Penny's Song First Annual Gala and Fundraiser.

Later in the afternoon, Trish drove over to the little ranch, looking for Clay. She found him by the corral speaking with three of the older children who were hanging on his every word. "You got to keep the horse healthy by brushing him every day. If he worked hard, he's gonna have dust, dead skin and hair under his sweat. Brush him down with a strong hand. He needs his pores open and that massage is gonna keep his muscles from going lax. Keeps his tack clean, too. Don't want to have a horse getting any infections especially under his blanket and saddle."

Clay demonstrated how to properly groom Tux, one of the corralled horses, by using a body brush and currycomb. "After I'm through, you'll each get a turn, and then we'll use a water brush to wash old Tux down."

Trish stood about five feet away behind Clay. Once he caught sight of her and Meggie, he nodded and lifted the corners of his mouth before turning back to the kids. She waited and watched. Meggie, wearing a bonnet today to keep the sun off her face, was keenly alert after just waking from a nap. Horses fascinated her and she took everything in. When Tux whinnied, Meggie squealed with delight and nearly jumped out of Trish's arms. She tightened her grip immediately.

Clay turned and looked on with amusement. His smile, aimed at Meggie, dazzled. Whenever Clay looked at the baby with affection and appreciation, the way he seemed to do lately, a hollow ache churned in her stomach. She couldn't much blame him—Meggie was the sweetest little thing—but she wished her dang heart wouldn't bottle up in her throat whenever Clay paid attention to the baby.

She turned from Clay now, watching the children as they went about their daily chores. Many of them smiled and waved. Trish saw a real sense of community here. The week was nearly over and it was apparent the kids had jelled into a cohesive family.

Wendy strode up to say that Preston needed help in the general store. Trish interrupted Clay's grooming lesson to tell him to meet her there. And after spelling Preston, who had another commitment, Trish took over the duties at the store. Primarily, it amounted to straightening shelves and entertaining Meggie with colorful items that captured her curious attention.

Twenty minutes later, Meggie began a fussy jag. She didn't want to go into the stroller. She didn't seem tired, having just woken from a long nap. She squirmed in Trish's arms even as she showed her around the store, trying to entertain her with the toys on the shelves. Why wouldn't she stop crying? She didn't know why the baby was so upset. After rocking her with deep sways of her hips, singing her favorite songs and offering her a bottle, Meggie continued to fuss. She was in a mood.

When a ten-year-old boy named Henry strolled into the store, eager to spend his tokens, Trish was at a loss to help him. The baby's cries echoed against the wood beam walls and probably reached a wide range outside. Trish was sure everyone at Penny's Song was stuffing cotton in their ears right now.

"Shush, shush," Trish whispered desperately. Meggie moved to and fro restlessly against Trish's chest. She was afraid the baby would wiggle straight out of her arms. She'd read that if a baby wouldn't stop crying while holding her, then you might as well put her down to self-soothe. Self-soothe, now that was a concept.

Ha! Like *that* was going to happen.

Henry had his hands plastered over his ears, looking at Meggie as if she was an alien who'd sprouted green horns and wings. "I'm sorry, Henry."

Trish made a move toward the parked stroller by the counter and bumped right smack into Clay's unyielding chest. Heck, she almost bounced off him. "Oh, I didn't see—"

The baby's wails drowned out the rest of her words.

"Let me have her," he said. Somehow he'd stepped inside unnoticed and now stood beside her. His deep voice caught Meggie's attention. The second the baby saw him, she lunged and Clay caught her midway, entwining arms with Trish as they made the exchange.

It all happened so fast. One minute, Meggie was screaming blue murder and wrestling against her mother's chest, the next she was in Clay's arms, quieting down. Two hundred pounds of muscle, brawn and deadly good looks, coupled with her adorable nearly five-month-old baby, who seemed suddenly and magically mesmerized, was a little hard to take.

Trish sat on the stool behind the counter. "Wow."

Clay grinned. Meggie's tears were wet on her cheeks and he gently brushed them aside with his shirtsleeve. "There you go."

"Can I get my Tonka truck now?" Henry pointed to a shelf above his head. "I want that one."

Clay strode over to pluck the yellow truck off the shelf. "You worked hard today, Henry. Be sure to take good care of this."

"I will." The boy looked at Clay as if he could turn sand to gold.

"Give Mrs. Worth your tokens now."

Henry nodded and a few moments later, Trish found herself alone with Clay and Meggie.

"I feel betrayed." Trish reached up to curl a hand over Meggie's head and gave an adoring pat. "I couldn't get her to stop crying for the life of me. And then *you* show up."

"I have a way with women." Clay winked with a sly smile, trying to cheer her up.

"So don't beat myself up because you have a way about you that even babies can't resist?"

Clay covered Meggie's ears. "I'd like to have my way with you again." One brow lifted in a sinister arch as dark stormy eyes bored straight through her. "Seems to me, you started something last night behind the pool house…"

Tremors of excitement rushed through her body at the mention of their almost-illegal tryst. Last night, she'd dreamed about finishing what they'd started and her dream was definitely not G-rated.

"Clay," she said, breathless.

"Admit that you've been thinking about it, too."

Trish had just battled a frantic baby and lost and now here she was, turning to putty in Clay's hands. She was slowly softening to him. How could she not, watching the two of them together? She'd have a full-fledged Clayton Worth meltdown if she wasn't careful. She had to get her head back in the game and knew exactly how to do it. "I've been *thinking* about business all day. I've got the ball rolling, but there's one teensy-weensy thing that you have to do."

The baby grabbed a lock of Clay's hair at the base of his neck, closed her fist and tugged. It didn't seem to faze him. "Name it."

"A radio interview with Red Ridge local news."

His face pulled tight in a wince. His eyes narrowed to slits as he shook his head. "No."

She'd expected this reaction from him. "I wouldn't ask it of you, but with Clayton Worth's name behind Penny's Song, you'll pull in more interest and donations for the cause. Just think of all the money you can raise."

"I'm not a celebrity anymore. You know I like to fly under the radar now. Red Ridge is my home and the folks around here respect that. I'm through with that part of my life, Trish. I thought you understood that when I retired and came to live at the ranch."

"I do understand that. And that's why I didn't go to a major network news station. We'll do a local story to raise interest in Penny's Song in the county. The more recognition we get, the more funds we'll raise and the more children we can help."

Meggie crawled up Clay's shoulder and he turned to her. Her inquisitive blue eyes met with Clay's dark ones and an innocent toothless smile broke out on her face. A special moment passed between the two of them, baby and man, that stilled Trish's heart and brought a sliver of jealousy along with it. Her baby seemed enthralled by him.

Clay let the baby distract him for a few long moments, visibly taken with Meggie. Then he turned to her. "I don't want to do it."

"I know." Trish smiled with assurance. "But you will."

Clay sucked in a breath and gave a slow nod with no small measure of reluctance. "Darn it, Trish, it kills me when you make sense."

"I know that, too," she said with glee. "You need to be at the news station first thing tomorrow morning. I'll call you with details."

He scowled. "Great. I'd better get out of here before you sign me to a nationwide concert gig." He kissed the top of

Meggie's head, matter-of-factly, as if it were an everyday occurrence before handing her over. "Be careful of your mother, baby girl," he said. "She's tricky."

Trish laughed while Clay frowned his way out the door.

Seven

Clay pulled up to Suzy's house just as the crimson sun was setting, the last burst blazing through his windshield. His Ray-Bans deflected the glare as he sat in the car, staring at the front door. He removed his sunglasses, folded them and placed them in an overhead compartment. He stared at Suzy's house some more and when a bird chirped from the mesquite tree overhead, Clay tried to spot it through the branches.

His lips twisted with disgust when he realized what he was doing.

Stalling.

What the hell was going on with him anyway? Before Trish showed up, he'd known exactly what he'd wanted and how he would go about getting it. Suzy was the perfect choice for him. She'd been through a difficult divorce. Had her fill of a worthless husband and had cried many a night on Clay's shoulder. She was free now, as he would be soon, and she was like family. She fit. Clay had gone over the positives about

Suzy in his head a hundred times. He liked her. She was easy to be around. And she wanted kids.

Trish has a kid.

The thought niggled at him all day. She has a kid and damn, she was a stunner. It tickled him how easily Meggie took to him. How it seemed almost natural holding her in his arms. He didn't have much experience with babies. He figured he would get all the experience he needed when Tagg and Callie had their child. But Meggie was here now and he felt an uncanny connection to her. When she clung to his neck today and pierced him with her sweet baby blues, in that instant he knew he'd have moved the moon to make her happy.

Clay rubbed his forehead, his fingers massaging out tension over his right temple. Suzy was expecting him tonight. Clay had offered a month ago to take her to the annual cattlemen's dinner held in Red Ridge. It was something they both attended every year, a way of honoring the old-timers whose traditions and way of ranching were rapidly declining, being overtaken by technology. Suzy's father was going, too. Whenever they could, the three of them attended together.

What the hell. He got out and looked over the roof of his car. Suzy had just stepped out of her front door and he watched her lock it up before turning to him. The second she spotted him, a smile spread across her face. The same friendly smile she'd always had for him. She waved and came forward. She was pretty, no doubt about it, with long flowing dark hair and expressive amber eyes. A colorful flowing dress flounced as she walked toward him. But the second she reached him, her smile faded.

"What's wrong?" he asked immediately.

"Dad's not coming. He's not feeling well."

"What's the matter with him?"

"He's tired. He claims he's catching a cold and doesn't want to infect us."

"But you don't believe him."

Suzy shook her head. "No. I think it's more than that. He's been overly tired lately. He doesn't want me *nursing* him, which means he doesn't want me to butt in. He says he'll be fine in a couple of days and to go without him and have a nice time."

"You look worried, Suze."

"I'd be lying if I said I wasn't."

"You want to skip it? We don't have to go."

Suzy's head tilted to one side as she gazed up to him. "Dad would find out if I didn't go and it would aggravate him. I've got orders to report back to him, you know, with all the gossip about his cronies."

Clay chuckled. "Got it. We'll go, then. Don't worry, he's tough as they come."

Appreciation shone in her eyes as she touched her hand to his arm. "Thanks, Clay. I don't know what I'd do without you." She reached up on tiptoes to press a warm kiss to his cheek.

A few times when she'd done that, Clay had taken liberties in kissing her back. It had almost gotten hot and heavy once or twice, but he'd always been the one to back off. There was an unspoken truth between them, that nothing would go further until Clay was legally divorced. Maybe he was a fool not to take what Suzy offered, but it was how he rolled. The vows he'd taken meant something to him.

It hadn't been easy turning away a woman like Suzy. All this time, he thought it was because he was doing the honorable thing. He'd never been unfaithful to Trish, not even when he'd been roaring mad at her. But now, Clay wondered if there had been more behind it. Maybe friendship with Suzy was all there could ever be.

Clay led Suzy to the car and helped her get in, then drove off. The drive was pleasant, Suzy chattering about her father's stubborn nature, her job at the hospital and the apple cobbler she planned on baking tomorrow. She invited him to stop by after his radio interview with WRRN in the morning to share it with him.

Clay told her he might just do that.

They spoke about Callie's pregnancy and how she was doing and when the subject turned to babies, Suzy commented, "I know it's a sore subject, but I think what Trish is doing with Meggie is admirable."

Clay cast a quick glance her way, keeping one eye on the road. "Yep, it is."

Puzzled, Suzy asked, "Yep, it's a sore subject and mind your own business, Suzy, or yep, it's admirable?"

"Admirable," Clay said, focusing back on the road.

"So you're okay with Trish being here?" Suzy probed gently.

Clay blew out a breath. Suzy knew everything about his marriage breakup, except that Trish had accused him of cheating with her. He didn't know exactly why he hadn't told Suzy that—pride maybe, or just wanting to keep some private things private. He shied away from awkwardness; having Suzy and Trish both working at Penny's Song was awkward enough already.

"She's here for a reason, Suzy. You know that."

"But seeing her with a baby? That must have been hard on you."

"Took me a while to wrap my head around the whole thing, but I can't lay blame on either of them. What happened between me and Trish in the past has nothing to do with the situation now."

"So you don't think she'll stay on?"

The moment Suzy had invited him over for apple cobbler, Clay's mind shifted to a different morning scene. Trish waking up half-groggy before dawn, diapering the baby in the crib, while Clay got a pot of coffee going and warmed the baby's bottle. They'd take turns feeding Meggie as the sun came up. But those thoughts were quickly banished with reality. "No, she's got a life in Nashville and a child to raise. Her work is there."

Suzy sat back in the seat, visibly satisfied with his answer and peered out the windshield, saying nothing more about it.

They made a short evening of it, dining and sitting through a few speeches and then ducked out before dessert. Clay took Suzy home and walked her to the door. She lingered there for a moment, looking a little hopeful, inviting him inside for a drink, but Clay begged off. He had an early interview, he reminded her. He waited until he was sure she was safely inside her house before leaving for home.

He found himself driving past the main house and slowing the car when he reached the guesthouse. The parlor lamp was on. Trish was still up. He wondered if Meggie was, too, fussing or drinking her bottle with her pretty eyes drifting closed. A strong impulse pulled at him. Knock on the door. Finish what you started with Trish. And then be done with it.

Too damn tempting, he thought. Every nerve in his body wanted to give in to the temptation. He wanted to see Trish. Make love to her again.

But it wasn't real. They were not his family.

In all truth, the two females were only a signature away from leaving town for good. After the divorce he'd never see them again. He turned his car around and headed home. He had no reason to barge in on them tonight and confuse the situation any more than it already was.

Let sleeping dogs lie, was the saying.

And Clay would heed that advice.

For now.

"Mrs. Worth, are you okay?" Preston peered at her hand in horror. Trish looked on just as horrified. Blood covered her hand, ran down her arm and colored the floor of the general store in a string of red droplets. Wrapped peppermint candies lay across the ground among shattered glass.

"Oh! I, uh…" She stared at her hand, then at the mess on the floor. "The jar…broke."

"I heard the crash. Hang on, I'll get a towel." Preston raced around the counter looking for something to wrap her hand in, but when nothing immediately jumped out at him, he yanked his T-shirt over his head. "Here," he said, coming forward shirtless. Trish was amazed at his quick thinking. He pulled the material lengthwise and twisted it around her hand a few times stopping the blood from spurting out. Then he tied it.

He applied pressure, keeping his eyes on the injury. "Does it hurt?"

"No, not at the moment. I think I'm in shock. I didn't expect the jar to break. I knocked into it and it crashed to the floor. I just reacted by lunging for it and a chunk of glass came up."

"You're lucky it didn't sever your wrist. Looks like a pretty clean cut, though. You may not need stitches, but you should see the nurse." Blood oozed underneath the makeshift shirt bandage. "I'll walk you to the infirmary."

"Oh, uh…okay. I have to get Meggie."

Trish had momentarily forgotten about her. Luckily, she was in the stroller, facing in the opposite direction. Preston strode over to the baby and nodded positively.

"She's fine. No glass anywhere near her."

"Thank God." Trish sent up a silent prayer of thanks.

"Hold your hand up. I'll get the stroller and we'll walk slowly. You're not feeling dizzy, are you?"

Trish shook her head. She'd lost blood, but not enough to make her dizzy, thank goodness. "Nope, I'm not dizzy, but I feel stupid."

"It was an accident," Preston said, reassuring her. "And they happen all the time."

Trish was grateful Preston was with her. He kept her calm and took over when she might have panicked. "You're good in an emergency."

"Thanks." He helped her outside while pushing the stroller. "I know first aid."

"You should be a doctor."

Preston sent her a sheepish smile. "I'm pre-med. So thank you for that."

That made sense. Most of the volunteers here had a propensity to nurture and heal. That's why Penny's Song was as good for the caregivers as it was for the children who'd come here. "Now I know why your nose is in the books all the time. You're going to be a great doctor, Preston."

Trish felt a little weak as she moved, but she forged on. When they got to the infirmary, near the main floor of the bunkhouse, she spotted Suzy in her white lab coat, looking professional. With a silent groan, Trish realized she was going to have to deal with Suzy at some point, but she never envisioned it would be in an emergency situation. The second she spotted her, Suzy's gaze went straight to the injury, her bloody bandaged arm bent at the elbow.

Suzy rose from the small counter she sat behind. "What happened?"

"Glass cut," Preston said, stepping up. "Nothing severed, but a deep-enough gash."

"Okay, have a seat," Suzy ordered calmly. "I'll take a look at it."

Trish sat facing her, her arm on the counter. She found herself shaking a little. "Preston, will you get Mrs. Worth a glass of orange juice from the saloon, please."

Preston parked the stroller so that Meggie faced both of

them. She seemed content, oblivious to the injury her mother suffered. "Sure, I'll be right back."

Suzy looked up and assured her, "You've lost some blood. That'll make you a little weak. The juice will help."

She put on a pair of gloves and carefully removed the T-shirt from Trish's hand, then cleaned the blood away with gentle jabs of cotton-soaked peroxide. "Looks like Preston was right. You're lucky it's not worse."

"I'll have to buy him a new shirt," Trish said, feeling guilty. The shirt he used as a bandage would never be worn again. "I'm glad he was there. He's a fast thinker."

"Yes." Suzy nodded, intent on her task. Trish took a second to study Suzy while she worked on her hand. She had long dark hair that was pulled back now at the nape of her neck in a ponytail that flowed down the white lab coat. Her complexion was creamy and blended perfectly with tawny amber eyes. She had an expressive face that couldn't hide emotion well—the open book kind of face that laid her emotions on the line—giving her away, time and time again when she looked at Clay. Trish had hated knowing that, *seeing* that, when no one else seemed to notice.

Meggie squawked and Trish tried to quiet her. "It's okay, sweet baby. Hush now."

Meggie wiggled uncomfortably, her body taking a long restless stretch. Soon she'd get antsy and want some attention.

"We'll be through here in a minute, Trish."

"I hope Meggie can hold on. She's been in the stroller awhile now."

Suzy dressed the wound, then bandaged her hand very tightly with layers of gauze. "It wouldn't hurt to have the wound looked at by a doctor when you're in town. You won't need stitches, but it's lengthy and might need further attention."

"All right, thank you." Trish tested her hand, splaying her

fingers. The wound angled above the inside of her right wrist and just below her thumb. The bandage seemed to do the trick by stopping the bleeding and allowing her some mobility.

She found Suzy looking at the baby with warmth and longing in her eyes. "She's sweet. I can't wait for one of my own. I heard you let Helen watch her the other night and she did fine."

"You know about that?" Trish blurted. She didn't want her mind to go there, to believe that Clay had spoken to Suzy about their intimate interlude at the hotel.

"Oh," Suzy said, taken aback. "I'm sorry. Clay told me last night that you'd driven over to the Ridgecrest Hotel to speak with the manager and Helen watched the baby while you were gone."

Last night? Clay had been with Suzy last night? That was all she heard of Suzy's explanation. Trish had trouble breathing. Her chest grew tight and raw hot anger bubbled up from her stomach. Damn it. She was still married to Clay for all intents and purposes. "Let me guess, you made white chocolate raspberry cupcakes sprinkled with nuts and cherries."

Suzy blinked, then sent her a glare.

Trish glared back.

"You hate that Clay is my friend."

"And you hate that he married me."

Suzy's face flamed, but it couldn't have been any hotter than the slow burn that scorched her own.

"That didn't work out so well, did it?"

Suzy's comment slapped at her rational senses. She forced the stiffness from her shoulders and rose from her seat. If she was still shaky, she was too angry to notice. "How kind of you to point that out."

Suzy rose as well, bustling about, cleaning up the counter and putting things away. "I'm sorry," she said finally, meeting her eyes. "That was…awful to say."

Trish couldn't disagree.

"I went through a bad divorce and Clay was the rock that held me together. We've always been close. We have roots here in Red Ridge. He and I, we're cut from the same cloth. The truth is, I've waited a long time for Clay. You had your chance. You walked out on him."

"I had reason."

"I'm sure you did. And it's none of my business, but what's done is done. You're getting a divorce and when you leave town again, Clay will be free."

Trish couldn't really argue with that. "He's not free, *yet*."

"He knows that and so do I." It was a statement made flatly, but in earnest and maybe with a touch of regret. "I'm not the reason you two broke up."

No, but she was a catalyst *and* the last straw. Trish held her anger in check. She read between the lines and saw the truth in Suzy's unflinching confession. Clay had been honest with her. He hadn't betrayed her with Suzy. If he had, Suzy would have let it slip, if not by actual words, but by her candid facial expressions.

"I'd better go." Trish turned to get Meggie. "She's going to need a bottle soon." Gripping the stroller with her left hand and leaning her body into it, she pushed it past Suzy and then turned. "Thank you," she said, gesturing with her bandaged hand. "For taking care of this."

"It's what I do," Suzy said with a shrug, her usual bright smile gone. She stood, her body rigid, but softness filled her eyes as she spared another glance at Meggie. "You're fortunate to have her, Trish."

"I know."

"She's going to fill your life with joy."

"She already does."

The yearning in Suzy's voice made Trish uncomfortable. This wasn't tit for tat. You get Meggie and I get Clay. But in essence, that seemed to be what Suzy was saying in a quietly desperate way.

"I can make Clay happy," Suzy said with a whisper. "Once you're gone."

Trish blinked. *Was she kidding?* Was she asking permission or did she want her approval? No way. No how. She'd be waiting until hell froze over, if that was the case.

And suddenly, Trish wasn't so sure that Suzy could ever make Clay happy. She wasn't sure of anything anymore. But Trish knew that she'd made Clay happy once and she was bound and determined to prove that to herself and to Clay.

For the little time she had left in Red Ridge.

The sound of Clay's boots scraping concrete brought a thrill to her heart. Trish peeked out the corner of the parlor window as he approached the front door. Moonbeams guided his way. His Stetson sat low on his forehead and shadowed the top half of his face concealing his eyes, making him look ominous and a little dangerous. She wondered what she would see in his eyes when she opened the door?

Trish blew out a breath. Determined to see this through, she walked to the entrance. Meggie was comfortably asleep in the play yard in the second bedroom. She wouldn't know Clay was here and if all worked out as she planned, he would be gone before she woke up in the morning.

She'd called Clay this afternoon, asking him to come over to work on the fundraiser tonight, after Meggie fell asleep. And Meggie, right on cue, conked out after her 8:00 p.m. bottle.

Perfect.

Country music played softly in the background. Trish had to grin. Just a minute earlier, Clayton Worth's first hit filled the airwaves and helped put little Meggie to sleep. His voice had matured since, but "Losing Out on Love," the song that skyrocketed Clay to fame when he was eighteen, was still a fan favorite. Now, Josh Turner's baritone voice carried through the house.

Trish waited for Clay's second knock, bolstering her courage, before answering the door. On a rocky breath, she pulled open the door with her good hand and hid her injured hand behind her back. "Hello, Clay."

Clay took one look at how she was dressed and raised an eyebrow. Appreciation shone in his expression. Seeing that look on his face helped boost her confidence, but Trish wasn't a natural flirt. She didn't play games. Maybe she shouldn't have come to the door wearing a red halter sundress that dipped into a vee in front and exposed enough skin in the back, edging just inches above her derriere, to tempt a saint.

"Trish."

He stepped inside, walked past her and turned abruptly. She caught him eyeing the back of her dress. Then he slid a long hungry look down her legs to her bare feet and red-painted toenails. His eyes shot up to hers. "You expect me to work with you looking like that?"

Busted. She'd deliberately dressed for seduction.

With her good hand, Trish smoothed out the lines of her dress, a motion Clay noticed with a quick snap of his head. He didn't miss a move she made. "Well, uh, I thought we could have a drink before we started. If you come into the parlor, I've got some papers you should look over."

"Liar."

"What?"

A broad smile whipped across his handsome face. "You want sex."

"What? I, uh..."

Clay moved on her like a tiger stalking his prey. His hat shadowing his eyes, he came to within inches from her face. "You want me."

Trish fluttered her eyes closed. Oh, boy.

"I bet you've got nothing on, underneath that dress."

Busted again.

"Let me see your hand," Clay ordered, but with enough sugar in his tone to make her comply.

"My hand?" A tremor of annoyance zipped through her body. So, the darn Suzy pipeline hadn't failed. She'd spoken to Clay today about her accident. "How did you know about it?"

"I ran into Preston today." He put his hand out palm up and she set her injured hand in his.

"Oh." So Suzy hadn't gone running to him with the news of their conversation. Relieved, she relaxed as much as she could under the circumstances. She wasn't coy or clever and Clay had seen right through her ploy.

"Does it hurt?" he asked as he examined her hand.

"It's more annoying than anything." Which was the truth.

He nodded, then looked toward the hallway leading to the bedrooms. "And Meggie's sound asleep?"

Trish smiled. "In the other bedroom. Yes."

Clay took her injured hand and brought it to his lips. He kissed each of her fingers gently on the tips. "I'm glad you weren't hurt."

She felt a pang in her chest. On a man like Clayton Worth, *tender* looked really good. And despite his tenderness, or because of it, she wanted to rip his clothes off. Trish saw her opportunity—she wouldn't pass it up—now was her chance.

She'd had a change of heart after hearing Suzy's parting comments today. No one was going to make her husband happy but Trish, not while she was still here in Red Ridge. Suzy wouldn't have the upper hand. Not this time.

Trish enjoyed having sex with Clay, so why shouldn't she indulge a little? They were still legally married and with that came wifely rights. Heaven knew, when she returned to Nashville, she'd be too busy juggling work and single motherhood to have any kind of romance in her life.

Meggie was asleep. Trish had hours to be alone with Clay.

"No, I'm not hurt. And yes, I'm not wearing anything under this dress. And yes, I don't give a damn about work tonight. I want you, Clayton Worth. *Bad.*"

She yanked the hat from his head and flung it.

Clay's eyes darkened to a gleam. His demeanor changed. The smile faded and his body reacted. He wrapped his hands around her waist and pulled her in. "You don't have to work so hard at it, honey. I'm all yours."

That had been true once, but Trish knew he was speaking only about tonight.

"I'm damn glad you made the effort, though."

Trish reached around his neck and pulled his head down, then lifted on tiptoes to plant a hot kiss on his mouth. Her lips burned with his heat. Her fingers dug into his hair. She sifted through the dark strands. Thick locks slipped through her fingers. Clay's groan of desire fed her confidence. She pressed herself closer, brushing her body to his. Their tongues found each other and the kiss went deep and long.

"Make love to me," Trish whispered between clashing tongues.

A rumbling emanated from the bottom of Clay's gut, the sound she knew meant *hell yeah.*

She ended the kiss abruptly, climbing off Clay's body. She took his hand and led him to the big comfortable master bed. The covers were turned down. Filled wineglasses sat on the nightstand and candles flickered next to them. "Right here, Clay. Right now."

She shoved Clay down and he went easily, his smile wicked as his body filled the length of the bed. She wouldn't pretend to think she could push him anywhere he didn't want to go, but she *would* have control tonight.

"If I'm dreamin'," Clay rasped low as Trish yanked off one boot, then another, "don't wake me."

"You're not dreaming. This is real." She spread his legs wide and climbed onto the bed between them. Lowering down to his level, she positioned her body over his, wrapped her arms around his neck and took him in a sweeping passionate kiss. Heat rose up her body in waves. Ripples of desire consumed her. She had Clay at her mercy and she would take advantage. She would make him happy. She didn't understand why the validation was important to her, but deep inside, she had to know that their marriage hadn't been a complete failure. There had been love and lust involved, despite the heartache and disappointment.

Her tongue danced with his, their mouths mating in fiery wet kisses. Little moans escaped her throat, her body electric as Clay returned her passion. Yet, he held back just enough to give her control. She wouldn't disappoint. She planted tiny kisses all over his mouth, then moved on to his chin. She suckled his strong jaw leaving him moist there. With her lips bowed, she blew at the moisture. Clay took a sharp swallow of air and stilled his entire body. She could see his desire, the restraint that made him wince as if he were in pain. Next, she followed along his neck with tiny nibbles until she reached the base of his throat. She licked him there and he made a triumphant groan.

She made fast work of unbuttoning his shirt. Her hands slipped under his shirt and she spread it out wide. His shoulders were muscled and strong under her palms. She loved touching him, feeling his strength, the power of his body. She gazed at him through candlelight and sucked in oxygen, relishing his body, memorizing it and savoring every morsel of him.

She ran her hands along his shoulders, then angled in over the full expanse of his chest. Tracing her fingers across his two nipples, his skin prickled. He groaned and moved on the bed, restless, arching with a buck, wanting to take control, but she shook her head and shoved him down gently. She couldn't let him have it. Tonight was about pleasing him. Making a point. And having a wildly wicked time. "Sit back and enjoy."

His dark eyes blackened even more and a slow grin spread across his face. "Done."

Trish smiled and continued touching him, tracing her fingers over his body with infinite precision. His skin was rougher than hers and her caresses did as much damage to her as they did to him. He was, in a word, perfect, as far as sexy hunks were concerned. And tonight, he was all hers.

Trish slid back on him enough to unfasten his belt buckle. She pulled at the belt and it fell open. She found the zipper to his jeans and looked at him while she slowly guided the zipper down, inch by inch.

"You're asking for trouble," he warned.

"You catch on quick." Tonight was all about taking risks and chances. Trish had always guarded herself. She'd always protected her heart. She wouldn't do that today. She wouldn't deny them this pleasure. Tonight she was asking for trouble and getting it. She worked him out of his jeans. His boxers came next and then she lowered her head and lifted her lashes to him as she gripped him.

A wicked gleam entered his eyes.

She tasted him with her tongue.

His body pitched.

"Damn it," he gritted between his teeth.

Then she took him into her mouth. A low guttural growl rumbled from his throat as he drove his hands into her hair. He guided her, showing her without words what he liked. She already knew. She pleasured him until he bucked beneath her ministrations and uttered a tortured groan. This time the warning in his voice was very real. He had his limits and so did she. She quaked inside, as her anticipation grew.

She lifted her head, only to be captured by the hungry glint in his eyes.

He slid his hands from her hair and unfastened the knotted ties of her halter top. With sure fingers, he finessed the ties, lowering them past her shoulders with achingly slow speed. His fingertips probed her with the gentlest touch and every ounce of her sensitive flesh jumped. When he touched her like that, she split apart. He cupped her breasts with his palms and she stilled, the heat in her belly burning hot. Moisture pooled between her legs and she fought the release that was building in her without her consent.

She had more to do.

She cupped her hands over his as he toyed with her breasts, showing him what she liked this time. He knew and the heat intensified until she could barely take it.

Then he shoved her hands away and brought his mouth up to suckle her with his tongue.

Oh, yeah. Clay knew what she liked.

"Let go, sweetheart." Clay's urging tempted her to take her pleasure now.

"No, not yet." She shook her head and rose up over him onto her knees. Lifting her dress, the material that had bunched at her waist now flowed over both of them.

Candlelight glittered onto the bed and tall shadows danced on the wall. The scent of red wine permeated the room. She wanted this to last. She wanted to create a memory. She wanted perfection. "There's more."

Clay's lips curved into a wicked smile. "Show me."

"Reach into the drawer and pull out a few packages," she whispered, nearly forgetting about the condoms she'd bought today.

"A few?" Clay choked back his question.

"At least," she murmured.

When he figured out she was serious, his expression changed and an approving gleam shone in his eyes.

Seconds later with the protection in place, she positioned herself over his thick erection, teasing the tip with the folds of her skin. She brushed over him once, twice, and he cursed. But Clay wasn't a slacker. He fought back and he had weapons in his arsenal that could render Trish helpless. His hand sought her entrance and with his finger, he stroked her sensitized flesh until she nearly lost all control.

She moved on him and he moved on her. There was a rhythm to their lovemaking, a beauty to the give and take. Clay kept the pressure constant as Trish lowered down on him. She rode the wave of their bodies arching and descending, taking him inside her deep, deeper. The slow erotic rhythm she created tortured them both as she seesawed on his erection, up and then down.

He rubbed her flesh again and again. Hot embers ignited and the flames grew until a fire raged like an inferno. Sizzling heat engulfed her. Sexy, desperate words ripped from Clay's mouth, encouraging her, praising her. He was as far gone as she was. She stretched her body back in a full arch, her hair catching air and flying past her shoulders. He gripped her hips and helped her take the hard deep ride. Her eyes slammed shut, but brilliant, dazzling lights appeared in them. "Clay!" she cried.

"Damn…" His voice was hoarse and desperate. He rasped out lusty commands that filled her mind and she answered him with her body, taking them both on the wildest ride of their lives.

Their orgasm burst like a rocket, the countdown fully synchronized and perfectly timed. Shudders racked Clay's body visibly and she opened her eyes in time to see the tormented pleasure on his face, to see admiration fill his eyes and the beauty that was his body, fully sated.

The landing was easy and gentle. They came down together exhausted.

Trish relaxed on Clay and he kissed the top of her head.

She clung to him as he clung to her.

They were quiet for a time, then Trish sat up and began to rise from the bed. Clay reached out to tug at her hand before she made it off the mattress. "Where are you going?"

"To check on the baby," she said.

He lifted up. "I'll come."

Immediately, she shook her head. "Stay. Wait for me. I'll be back soon."

Clay stared at her for a brief moment and then nodded. He lay down on the bed and watched her put on her robe and pad out of the room.

Trish staggered against the wall in the other bedroom and braced herself. That had been incredible. Her body still hummed to Clay's beat. She was complete for the moment, but her hunger for Clay hadn't fully ebbed. She still wanted him, wanted more of the exquisite sensations running through her system. She wanted to overload on him and have him overload on her.

It was going to be a great night, with no holds barred.

She peered at Meggie who was just rousing. It was time for a diaper change and a bottle. She watched the baby wake, the beginning of awareness as she scooted around looking for comfort until her eyes snapped open and she realized she was alone.

Before she let out a peep, Trish approached the playpen. "I'm here, baby girl."

Meggie's face scrunched up. She was wet and hungry and ready to let go a wail of frustration. "No, no. Shush, sweetheart."

She bent to pick Meggie up and cuddled her to her chest. The baby surrendered immediately, taking the comfort and love she offered. At that moment, Trish felt an alarming sense of not only peace but of completeness. With Clay lying in the room next door and Meggie in her arms now, Trish had it all and the hollow ache that followed warned her not to go there. She *didn't* have it all. It was an illusion.

Red Ridge wasn't her home.

Clay wasn't her man…much longer.

As long as she remembered that, she'd do fine.

She diapered Meggie without fuss and replaced her slightly soiled pajamas with a pair with cute little brown and yellow animals on them. She carried Meggie into the kitchen to warm her bottle. While she waited for the pot to heat, she sat with Meggie in the parlor and rocked her gently, humming a lullaby.

A shadow caught her eye and she turned. Clay leaned casually against the wall, dressed only in his jeans, arms and feet crossed, watching her. They stared at each other, then Clay's eyes drifted to the baby.

It was a beautiful sight, seeing the warmth overflow in his eyes, seeing the yearning there as he looked at her daughter. It was a moment, a brief interlude in time where all things were possible and imaginable.

But Trish put a halt to that thinking. She hadn't come to Red Ridge to get Clay back. She'd come for the opposite reason. Nothing had been resolved between them. Not one thing. She hated to mar this moment with harsh reality, but it cruelly stared back at her regardless. Her heart took a tumble. Her time here with Clay had nothing to do with Meggie. She should have known she couldn't have avoided this. The guest-house was small and her plan had flaws. But as soon as she left town, Clay would move on with his life.

Tomorrow Trish would phone her Realtor and set her

future plans in motion. Spending time with Clay could only be a brief interlude before her new life truly began.

She felt some relief when Clay walked into the kitchen. It gave her time to regroup and forget the protective glint she witnessed in his eyes when he looked at Meggie. She tightened her hold on the baby, continuing to hum, rocking her back and forth gently.

Minutes later, Clay returned with the warmed bottle. He sat down next to her quietly and handed it to her.

"Thanks," she whispered.

He swept her hair from her throat and kissed her there. "You're welcome."

Tingles danced along her nerve endings.

"Put her down in her crib when you're through," he said softly, stroking Meggie's head.

Meggie glanced at him, curious, but when Trish put the bottle near her mouth, all curiosity faded and she became eagerly intent on sucking the formula dry.

Trish had put Meggie down in the play yard, where she normally napped, so that she could have a few hours with Clay in the master bedroom. She'd felt a little guilty about it, although the baby slept well in both beds, but Clay had recognized what she'd done and wanted Meggie to have her own bed for the rest of the night.

Trish nodded and felt immeasurably closer to Clay because of it.

Meggie fell back asleep after her feeding and Trish carried her to the master bedroom. Clay followed and watched her lay the baby down. He blew out the candles that had melted halfway down and picked up the wineglasses. He left the room and Trish found him in the kitchen, waiting for her.

"She's out again."

Clay smiled. "That a girl." His hair was rumpled due to her probing fingers. The early hint of a day-old beard divided his face from jawline to cheek, making him look even sexier, if that were possible.

Clay handed her a glass of wine and she took one sip. Her days of drinking anything more than an infinitesimal amount of alcohol were over. She was a single mother now and had to keep her wits about her day and night for the baby. She didn't need booze to make her want Clay. He was sex in a bottle and they'd always gotten drunk on each other.

This memory would stay close to her heart because when she got back to Nashville, her life would shift in another direction entirely, centered around Meggie and her work. She wouldn't have time for men. She couldn't even fathom letting someone get close again. Trish grew up not trusting in others much less the ones who claimed to love you.

She turned to rinse out the bottle at the sink rather than drool over her husband and feel things she had no right feeling anymore. It was a screwy set of circumstances that was starting to really confuse her.

Clay came up from behind, tucking her head on his shoulder and pulling her close as his body met hers through their nightclothes. "What are you doing now?" he asked.

Right away, the confusion cleared. She wasn't going to overthink her actions tonight. She would go with the flow and heed the desire that she couldn't deny. Without hesitation, she turned in his arms and untied her robe. His eyes drifted to her naked body. "You." She kissed him softly, her mouth lingering, whispering over his warm lips. "I'm going to do you, again."

His laugh was deep and husky as he bent her back and glanced at the granite counter with a sinister arch of his brow. "Any particular place in mind?"

"Your choice this time, but I get the next."

Then she draped her arms around his neck and clung on.

Eight

"You can't be serious about this," Trish said to Clay, her nerves jumping.

"You've gotta stop worrying so much." He sat on a big sorrel cutting horse named Thunder. The gelding was huge. His name alone brought fear into her heart. How had she let Clay talk her into this?

He reached down for Meggie and Trish wanted to take the baby and make a run for the hills. "Hand her up to me."

"You're sure?" She kept her voice down and Meggie plastered to her chest. Trish didn't want to argue with Clay or undermine his authority in front of the children. She glanced back at all of their eager faces as they sat on their horses, waiting to leave the corral area behind. This was the third group of "ranch hands" to come to Penny's Song in the three weeks since she'd been here. And each group of kids she'd met had taken an instant liking to Meggie. They were thrilled that she was taking a ride along the Red Ridge path with them. "I mean, she won't fall or anything, will she?"

Clay cut her a sharp look but kept his tone light. "You trying to insult me, honey?"

"No, of course not," she whispered, quickly shaking her head.

"I've been riding since I was three. I *ride* better than I walk. Isn't that a fact, Wes?" Clay glanced at his foreman who was right beside them, helping an eight-year-old girl named Melinda onto a mellow chestnut mare.

"That's right. The baby will be safe with Clay," Wes called over to Trish. He tightened the cinch on the saddle and adjusted the stirrups to the child's size. "That gelding knows who's boss, too."

"You see?" Clay sent her a satisfied nod. "She's gonna be in the sling thingy anyway. You said yourself, it's sturdy. And you're gonna be riding right next to me."

Trish knew all that. She trusted Clay. He was an expert horseman, but her nerves still bounced. She felt an incredible sense of responsibility with the baby and worried herself sick over things. Clay told her she ought to let Meggie experience something new, in the BABYBJÖRN atop a horse. "Okay."

With trepidation, she handed Meggie up to him. The baby went all too willingly. The two were getting closer by the day. And Trish hadn't been able to stop it. Her plan to keep Meggie and Clay apart had proven hopelessly impossible. They were both around Clay a great deal of the time, and it was clear that he thoroughly enjoyed being with the baby.

Each day they'd go about their business, Clay working at Worth Ranch, and Trish working on the fundraiser. Some afternoons they'd meet at Penny's Song where Clay would oversee the facility and make sure all was running right. Trish spent her time at the general store. She enjoyed keeping the place up, interacting with the kids. It was the best-suited job for a woman with a baby.

On the days Trish didn't see Clay, she was thinking about

him. And in the evenings when he would come over, they'd wind up in bed, making love half the night.

Trish understood that this affair, fling or whatever it was between them, was temporary, yet the past three and a half weeks had been pretty glorious. She had a few days left in Red Ridge until the Penny's Song fundraising gala. She'd leave for Nashville a day to two later. Her life had to get back on track.

Clay managed Meggie into the carrier that was strapped over his shoulders. "Here, better cover her head." Trish handed a bonnet up. Meggie didn't squawk when Clay fastened the ties. Meggie was ready to go, but Trish wasn't sure she was. She mounted her mare and with Wes and two other volunteers, Clay led the group on a tour of the property.

Meggie kicked her legs out, thrilled to be atop the horse. She babbled incoherent words, but the excitement in her voice was easy enough to understand.

"She's loving this," Clay said, smug.

"Mmm." Too much, Trish thought. Clay looked natural with a baby plastered to his chest, riding his horse. It was a hard scene to watch because they'd be leaving soon and Meggie wouldn't have Clay's chest to curl up into at night anymore. She wouldn't hear his baritone voice lulling her to sleep or have his strong arms rocking her when all else failed.

Meggie was falling for Clay and it was the last thing she wanted. But Trish's fears multiplied when she thought Meggie wasn't the only one. If she probed deep into her heart she'd find the same was true of her. Instead of mulling that over until her head ached, she sucked in a fresh breath and tried to enjoy the children and the Red Ridge landscape.

Halfway into the ride, Clay caught her attention and pointed his chin down at Meggie. Trish's gaze lowered to her. She found her fast asleep, her head slumped and bobbing gently against Clay's chest. He put his hand there to straighten her head and give her a pillow as she slept. "You want to ride back?" he asked quietly.

"I think the fresh air and altitude knocked her out. We probably should."

On a nod, Clay turned the horse, spoke a few words to Wes and the other volunteers and Trish followed Clay back to Penny's Song. Once at the stables, Clay dismounted, his naturally smooth moves keeping her daughter sound asleep in the BABYBJÖRN. Trish dismounted her mare and took the reins of both horses leading them to Travis, one of the older children who'd assumed the role of stable hand. "If you wouldn't mind," she said. "I've got to get Meggie home."

"Sure thing, Mrs. Worth. I'll take good care of the horses."

A few minutes later, Clay had Meggie safely secured in the car seat and she hadn't missed a beat. She still slept soundly.

"I'll see you tonight," he said.

"Oh, uh, can't tonight. I'm having dinner with Callie."

Clay pursed his lips with a hint of a frown. "A girls' night out?"

"Yep, no boys allowed. Just me, Meggie and Callie." Trish tried to make light of it, but she was grateful that she could put some space between them. They'd grown closer these past few weeks and yet neither one of them had spoken about their feelings for each other. As far as she knew, their relationship was all about making up for lost time, *sexually*. And nothing more.

"Gotcha." Clay stole a glance at Meggie one last time, the warmth in his eyes undeniable. Then he turned to Trish. "Try not to have too much fun. I'll see you tomorrow."

He tipped his hat and then pivoted on his heel and strode away. Trish watched him go, his shoulders broad and straight as an afternoon shadow followed him. He looked larger than life, but then Clay always had been, she mused. He'd been a star, a man comfortable in his own skin, a man who'd had the world laid out at his feet. He'd achieved all he'd set out to accomplish in life. Except for one thing—he'd wanted children and Trish had been the woman to deny him. She'd also questioned his honor in their marriage and made him see his flaws. In short, she'd been a burdensome bump in his very smooth road.

As he reached the bunkhouse, Suzy Johnson came up to greet him. They laughed about something, Suzy tossing her head back, her eyes fastened to Clay's. She touched her hand to his arm as they walked away together. Trish's heart grew heavy with sorrow. Once Trish was gone from the ranch, Suzy would step right into Clay's life without making any kind of ripple. She wouldn't cause him an iota of trouble. She'd slide into place beside him and give him everything he wanted.

Trish was beyond jealousy now. Regret ate at her. She surrendered to it and tears welled in her eyes. A painful thought nagged at her and the same old feelings of rejection and betrayal haunted her. Seeing Suzy with Clay brought her a sterling picture of her own future. Her heart crumbled as she finally faced the hard truth.

You don't belong here.
You never did.

They played poker for pride, more than anything else. Since the inception of Penny's Song, whenever Tagg, Jackson and Clay got together it was sibling rivalry at stake and bragging rights. Whoever won the pot in the end donated the money to the family charity anyway. Penny's Song always came out the winner, so Clay usually didn't mind playing with his brothers.

But tonight his head wasn't in the game and it was apparent by the lack of chips on the table in front of him. He was losing.

He brought a shot glass to his lips and sipped. He felt the slow burn of whiskey in his throat but it didn't numb the uneasy feeling in his gut. Something was up with Trish today. She seemed different and all too eager to send him away. Not that he'd spent every night with her, but many of them. They'd had some good times together using the pretence of working on the fundraiser to see each other. But soon, she'd be gone and Clay would move on from there.

"Your move, bro," Tagg said. "You betting or what?"

"Hang on," he said, ignoring the impatience in his brother's voice. Clay stared at his cards. He held a pair of eights. Not the best hand, but Clay was in a hell of a mood and didn't give a damn about winning. He made a bet, pushing in half his chips.

When had he *not* cared about winning?

Jackson went all in, which would wipe Clay out, if his eights didn't hold. He shoved in the rest of his chips.

Jackson tossed his cards face-up showing a spade flush to Clay's measly pair. His brother curled his lips in a triumphant smile as he raked in his winnings. "You're playing sucker poker tonight."

"Yeah, what's up with you?" Tagg asked. "You're tight-lipped tonight."

"I've got a lot on my mind with the gala coming up," he pointed out.

Tagg eyed him suspiciously. "Oh yeah, anything wrong?"

"Nothing's wrong." Except his life. The hell of it was, he thought he could pass off making love to Trish these past few weeks as pure lust. He'd purge her from his system and send her packing back to Nashville. Then he'd resume his uncomplicated life with Suzy. But damn it, it wasn't as easy as he thought.

Nothing about Trish was ever *easy*.

And that cute kid of hers? Meggie was innocent in all this

and Clay felt for her loss. She'd been orphaned. Somehow, that bundle of smelly diapers, stained bibs and ear-piercing cries had wormed her way into his heart. When Meggie's image flashed before him, all he saw was the big adorable smile she had for him. Saying goodbye to both females didn't sit well.

"If Trish's running the whole shebang, I bet it'll be a helluva night," Jackson commented.

"She is," Clay said, "and it will be. I have no doubts."

"So, after the gala, she's gone?" Tagg asked.

Clay polished off his whiskey, setting his glass down slowly. "Yeah, I suppose. It'll be over and done with." He stared at the shot glass in his hand.

Silence.

Finally, Tagg spoke up. "Okay, well, I guess we're done with poker. We can catch the tail end of the Diamondbacks game. Callie won't be home for another hour or two."

Clay lifted his lids. "How do you know that? You got her on a curfew or something?"

The jibe sailed right over Tagg as he reached into his pocket, pulling out his phone. "Technology is a beautiful thing." He read the screen silently. "Let's see…she's watching an old movie with Trish right now." Then with a sheepish grin, he added, "Texting is my new normal."

Jackson chuckled and the sound grated on Clay's nerves. "That's one way to keep track of your wife."

Tagg shook his head, taking the teasing in stride. Nothing got to him these days. He was "all in" with Callie and the happiest Clay had ever seen him. "Yeah, well, talk to me when your woman is carrying your child. Tell me you won't want to know how she's doing every minute of the day."

Jackson's mouth opened and then shut. Usually nothing stopped him from spouting off. "I'll take your word for it."

"Damn right." Tagg turned to Clay, changing the subject.

"Hey, I caught your interview on the radio the other day… pretty good, even if you sounded a little rusty."

Clay couldn't fault his brother's honesty. He *was* rusty and far removed from his celebrity days. He'd come back to ranching and the Worth empire at the right time in his life. "I'd rather be strapped to the grill of a ten-wheeler going eighty miles an hour than give an interview, but I couldn't say no to helping the charity. I took one for the team."

His brothers nodded.

Clay scraped his chair back and rose from his seat. He wasn't in the mood for small talk or poker or hanging out watching baseball. "Think I'll be going. Thanks for the game."

Tagg gestured with an elaborate wave of his hand to sit back down. "Stay put for one more minute."

"Why? What's up?"

Tagg poured two fingers of whiskey into all three shot glasses, then rose from his seat. Leaning forward he lifted his glass, his voice filled with pride. "I want to make a toast to my…son. We're having a boy. He'll be Rory Taggart Worth."

Jackson's mouth curled into his signature grin. "Hey, congratulations."

Clay lifted his glass in an air toast. "That's great news, Tagg. Dad would be honored."

"Yeah, he would have," Tagg agreed.

Clay sat back down. He needed that drink now. Not that he begrudged his brother any happiness. Tagg went through hell when his first wife died and now he had a second chance with Callie and a son to raise to adulthood. Tagg had paid the price and now was finally getting the life he deserved. But that didn't stop Clay's gut from grinding, though, or his head from throbbing. And it had nothing to do with Tagg or his future son.

Clay had failed his father. He couldn't grant him his dying

wish, a man he'd looked up to, a man he fully admired. When Clay made a vow, he kept it and this one had been the most important of his life. All this time, he'd blamed Trish for that. She'd been his scapegoat, the one he could point his finger at when he had a mind to determine fault. All this time, he hadn't forgiven her.

You made another vow, jackass. Just as important. To her. And he'd blown it.

The notion *blew* his mind. Had he failed Trish as well? He'd married her, promising to love, honor and cherish her. He'd always blamed her for what ailed their marriage. Now, Clay took a chilling hard look at his part in their breakup. Damn it. The clarity sucker punched him below the waist. He wasn't expecting this.

Why now? Why had he finally admitted it to himself?

Hell if he knew for sure.

Clay went home that night feeling like crap. He climbed the stairs to his bedroom and wrestled his way out of his clothes. Then he laid on the bed and poured one-hundred-dollar-a-bottle whiskey down his throat. Seeing the truth about himself was a hard pill to swallow and tonight Clay chose not to see it at all. His mind fuzzed out and his limbs gave way to the numbing effects of alcohol. Grateful for the peace, he fell into a dreamless sleep.

Morning was late in coming. Clay's head hurt like a son-ofabitch. He'd drunk himself silly last night, but lying flat on his butt was not an option. He had work to do, and judging by the sun's position on the horizon, he'd already burned enough daylight. Moving slowly, he lifted his head off the pillow. Pain shot through his skull, reminding him of his younger days of foolhardy drinking. Back then, staying upright had been a major accomplishment.

He shifted his feet onto the floor and leaned forward,

elbows braced on his knees. He rubbed his scalp. Piranha swam in his head and nipped at his brain. He swore up and down. He'd been an idiot.

His cell phone rang a tune; the sound of Kid Rock grated on every last nerve in his body. He sat on the bed and looked through the mess of clothes on the floor. He heard the sound in between his pants and socks. Constant jackhammering continued in his head. He grabbed for the phone and hurriedly slid open the screen, cutting off the blast of music. "What?"

"Uh, Clay, it's Raul Onofre from Southwest Bank."

Onofre was a friend from school who'd taught him how to read music and play guitar. They used to jam together. Now, Raul was his banker. "Did we have an appointment today?"

"No, no, nothing like that. But there's a little confusion I thought you might be able to clear up. I got a call from a lender in Nashville this morning. It seems that your wife, Trisha, is seeking a home loan from them. They're prequalifying her, but somehow the paperwork got to me for approval. I know the situation with your wife...uh, unless that's changed. Apparently, she's insisting that they not use your assets to qualify her."

Trish was buying a house? That was news to him. Oh, man. It took him a minute to process that. Anger filled his crowded head. He tried reasoning it away. He shouldn't be surprised that Trish would want to move Meggie into something bigger than an apartment. The kid deserved to live in a nice home.

Clay shut his eyes. A home in Nashville meant Trish was cementing their divorce. It meant she was moving forward and making a life without him. He knew this was coming. Yet the reality felt like a body slam to a brick wall. His brain felt too muddy to sort it out. Raul held on the line patiently.

"I appreciate the call, Raul. Truth is, I'm going to have to get back to you on this."

"You got it, Clay. Uh…everything else okay?"

"Yeah, just fine. Busy with the fundraiser. You're coming, right?"

He laughed. "Are you kidding? It's the biggest thing to happen in Red Ridge in a decade. After that stellar interview you gave, my wife would hang my hide if I didn't take her."

"All right. I'll see you then."

Clay hung up the phone. He'd sobered quickly. He had to face facts.

Trish and Meggie were leaving Red Ridge in three days.

Nine

Trish sat outside in the small Red Ridge café attached to the inn, wedged between an intricate iron fence covered with pink-hued azaleas and another café table. Calderone's was known for its stone-ground tortillas, to-die-for guacamole and margaritas made in seventeen different flavors. *Seventeen.* She would have liked to try just one today.

Meggie sat upright in her stroller, but her shelf life these days wasn't more than ten minutes. Unless of course, she'd fall asleep. But Trish didn't want her to sleep now. She wanted her wide-eyed and alert during lunch.

"He'll be here soon," she said to the baby. "I can't wait to see him."

"*He's* right here. Right on time."

Trish lifted her gaze to the familiar voice. "Blake!" She jumped up and wrapped her arms around her brother's neck. She squeezed tight and hung on. He'd come from California to meet Meggie and attend the Penny's Song gala. "Oh, I can't believe you're here. You're actually here."

"I told you I'd come."

"I know. I know. But it's been so long. And I've missed you."

"Missed you, too, sis."

They broke their embrace and she studied his face. She'd seen him looking healthy for years, but even now when she gazed at him, the boy with the sunken cheeks, bald head and stick-thin limbs still plagued her brain. It was as if she had to absorb his present good health and let it seep into her consciousness to make sure that little boy who'd almost died was alive, vital and healthy now.

"You haven't met Meggie yet."

"No, I haven't." He dropped down into a crouch and peered at the baby in the stroller. "Hey, hello there, beautiful. I'm your uncle Blake. And I plan on spoiling you rotten."

"You've already sent her a dozen toys."

He touched Meggie's hand, gazing at her for a moment with warmth in his eyes. Then he looked over his shoulder at her. "You're a mom now. I guess I had to see it to believe it."

He stood and she met his eyes with a tilt of her head. "I am. It's coming slowly, but I feel like a mother more and more now. I came about it differently than most women." She blinked her eyes several times. "I never do anything the normal way, do I?"

He nodded with a knowing smile. "You and me both."

It did her heart good to see him regard his past with earnest resignation. Blake didn't dwell. He had too much living to do and he'd always had a good attitude. Some say it's what kept him alive, made him healthy.

"So, you want to eat?" He pulled out the chair for her and together they took their seats. The waiter brought them chips and guacamole right away and two glasses of water.

During lunch they caught up on each other's news. Trish

was happy to note how well Blake's partnership was doing with GamerX, his up-and-coming video-game company, her brother being the designer extraordinaire of other worlds. Being alone in a hospital room away from everyday life had sparked his genius and imagination at a young age. While other kids were outside playing baseball, soccer or starting a rock band, Blake had been playing those games in his head and Trish would like to think his time in the hospital had not been wasted. It was all in the master plan. Now, he spent most of his time in California where his company was located or traveling the country to sell his ideas.

"I wasn't sure if you'd come," Trish said as she took the last bite of a veggie taco. Then she paused. "You've had enough illness in your life to last ten lifetimes."

"All the more reason. I can relate to the kids who have recovered and are ready to mainstream back. Just put me to work."

"Oh, I will. I hope you're all settled into the hotel because we're heading to Penny's Song right after our meal."

"Has Clay been working with you?"

"Yes, he has." Sensitive to her feelings, Blake hadn't brought up the impending divorce yet. "We do fine together," she assured him. "We're both committed to the charity, so there hasn't been a problem."

And now that Blake was in town, Trish's days and nights would be occupied. It was a blessing in some ways and it saddened her in others. Her secretive pre-divorce fling was over.

"Have you spoken to Mom and Dad lately?" he asked.

"I speak with Mom once a week. She seems to be enjoying Florida. I invited both of them to come, but they...they thought it would be awkward," she said with a shrug. "You know, with what's happening with the divorce. Do you talk to them often?"

Blake bit into a tortilla chip as he shook his head. "I travel a lot. When I'm home, I'm busy."

Her brother was holding something back. She could see it in his eyes and hear the trepidation in his tone. Suspicious, she asked, "What aren't you telling me, Blake?"

"No, nothing really. I, um, just need some space, that's all. We talk, but not like we used to. I'm over my illness and I'm tired of having to explain my health to Mom every time I get her on the phone. I just want to live a normal life."

She smiled sadly at the irony. Blake had the opposite problem with their parents than Trish did. While they worried themselves sick about him, they'd always relied on dependable, efficient Trish to take care of herself. Even now, her mother and father weren't making tremendous overtures to see Meggie, their new granddaughter. They offered to visit her next month sometime, but Trish wasn't holding her breath. "I get that, Blake. I do. They've always worried about you. It's almost like second nature now."

"I appreciate all they've done for me. I know the sacrifices they made." He turned a somber eye toward her. "And I know what my illness cost you, too."

"No, that's not true." She couldn't let him feel badly for something completely out of his control. "It didn't cost me anything. I'm just glad you survived, Blake."

He stared at her with a dubious expression but seemed to think better than to argue the point. The subject changed to something more pleasant, the new woman in Blake's life. Trish was grateful her brother had survived his childhood. His life was full now and she felt great satisfaction in that.

When the doorbell chimed at six o'clock, Trish was sure it was her brother right on time for dinner. She opened the door with a big smile, and came face-to-face with Clay. He stood stiff, like a plank of wood, his lips tight.

"Oh, uh, hello, Clay."

"Trish." Freshly showered and shaved, he looked groomed and dressed for a night on the town. The tantalizing scent of leather musk followed him as he swept his way inside the house. "Where's Meggie?"

An uneasy feeling stole over her. "In her playpen."

He glanced down for a moment as if summoning great patience and when he finally made eye contact, the intense look in his eyes made her shiver. "I want to talk to you."

"Uh, it's…it's not a good time." She had a feeling whatever he had to say shouldn't be said in front of Blake. "My brother's here. I mean, he's not here right now, but he's coming any second. He's in town for the—"

"You're buying a house in Nashville."

Surprised, she jerked her head back. How did he know that? Had Callie told him? She'd like to think her friend wouldn't repeat their conversations and betray her trust. "How did you find out?"

"Your lender called my bank for some information."

"And of course they pipelined it right to you." Clay had too many pipelines, she decided. But at least now she knew Callie could be trusted.

"I'm not the one secretly buying a house."

His overbearing tone rubbed her the wrong way. "It's not a secret, Clay. It just happened a little while ago." She lifted her chin. "Is there a problem?"

He glared at her like she was an idiot for even asking the question. "You should've told me."

She began shaking her head. "It's none of your… I'm not asking you for anything," she rushed out. "I'm doing this on my own."

Clay rolled his eyes, his tolerance looking pretty thin. "I don't give a damn about the money. If you need me to sign for something, I'd do it."

"I...don't. I can handle it."

"You always do, don't you?" His tone was sharp enough to cut glass.

She stared at him, baffled. She hadn't seen him today, but they had plans to go over the final arrangements for the gala, detail by detail tomorrow morning. What was he so burned about that it couldn't wait until then?

"I'm sorry...I don't know what you're getting at."

"Forget it," he said, obviously annoyed with her. He strode past her heading toward the second bedroom.

"Where are you going?"

He didn't answer. She followed him, stopping at the doorway to watch as he stood over Meggie's playpen. The baby jumped for joy the second she spotted him and reached her chubby arms up. Clay's hard expression softened. The tick that beat at his jaw smoothed to align with the plane of his face, and his broad stiff shoulders relaxed. Even his stance changed from rock solid to almost liquid.

"How's my little wildflower today?" he asked. Meggie responded by stretching her arms up even farther. Clay bent over the playpen and picked her up effortlessly. She cooed and looked at him with innocent trust that was dangerously sweet. It tore Trish to shreds.

Cradling her, Clay hummed a tune that had once caused his female fans to faint flat on the floor. Meggie was mesmerized and Trish was almost brought to her knees, too.

Heaven help her.

Trish took a hard swallow. Her eyes stung and she held back tears. She fought the retching emotion building up. She fought it tooth and nail. She fought it for all she was worth. Clay held her baby tenderly, with total affection, and it was obvious the two belonged together. They fit. The strong tall cowboy and the blue-eyed baby bundle somehow looked perfect together. Trish shut her eyes, denying the sensations washing over her, wishing them away with silent, heartfelt pleas.

Don't love him. Don't love him. Don't love him.

But she did. She loved Clay.

Stunned, she couldn't rationalize it away.

She *loved* her husband and she'd probably never stopped loving him.

The emotion sapped her strength. Everything went numb. She couldn't watch the two of them any longer. She turned away, squelching the feeling with stark willpower. Her pride being what it was, she held that emotion in check.

Blake's timing couldn't have been worse, or better, depending on how she looked at it, but he knocked then and she answered the door, giving her brother a cheerful smile, while her heart lay recklessly in danger of breaking.

Again.

"Hey, sis. The place looks nice," he said, entering the home and glancing around. "I remember you doing some remodeling here, if I'm not mistaken."

"You're not…mistaken. I, uh, enjoyed every second working on it," she replied, distracted. She needed to snap out of it. Right now. "Come into the kitchen. Dinner is almost ready. I hope you're hungry."

He followed her into the kitchen. "I shouldn't be, but I am."

"That's good," she said. Her appetite had vanished.

Clay walked into the kitchen holding Meggie on one arm. The baby took one look at Blake, then turned to Clay and clung to his neck, suddenly shy. Clay comforted her with a stroke of the hand and hugged her tighter before stopping a few feet from Blake. "It's good to see you, Blake," he said, putting out his free hand.

The two men shook. "Same here, Clay. You're looking well. And I see you've made friends with Meggie."

Clay slid Trish a sideways glance, then nodded. "She's a good baby."

"She's wonderful," Trish agreed without sparing him another look.

"Are you having dinner with us?" Blake asked.

Before Trish had a chance to offer an invitation, Clay shook his head to decline. That was a good thing. Her emotions were way out of whack. She couldn't deal with Clay and her unwelcome feelings right now.

"No, I've got plans for the evening."

Trish wondered where he was going, dressed so nice. It was better for her sanity that she didn't know.

Clay transferred Meggie into her arms. She went easily, accustomed to being shifted between the two adults in her life. Clay sent Meggie a lingering look before turning to Blake. "I hear the kids over at the little ranch had a ball with you today."

"Yeah, it was great for me, too. We relate to each other. Talk about been there, done that. That's me, a dozen times over." On a deep sigh, Blake went on, "What you and my sister are doing is a very good thing. I'm very impressed with Penny's Song."

"Thanks, I'm pretty darn proud of it," Clay said, then cut the conversation short. "Well, I'll see you around, Blake. We'll talk some more another time." He shot Trish a momentary glance before giving her a curt goodbye. "Trish."

As soon as the door closed, immense relief washed over her. She could breathe again, which was a task since her heart was in her throat.

"What was that all about?" Blake asked. "Clay couldn't wait to get out of here."

Tears hid behind her eyes. "I know."

She'd allowed the baby to get close to Clay and she'd never forgive herself for that. As for her, falling for him again was futile. She'd done the two things she'd vowed not to do because as much as she wanted to believe otherwise, Clay hadn't made any real overtures toward her. He hadn't claimed undying love. He hadn't asked her to stay in Red Ridge. For all she knew, he still harbored mistrust and resentment toward her. They'd had great sex and had shared some intimate evenings together. Period. She'd been a fool and now not only would she pay the price, but Meggie would, too.

She admonished herself and admitted to Blake on a barely audible whisper. "I've really messed up this time."

Trish sat across from Clay at the kitchen table sipping coffee discussing the details of the gala tomorrow night. For all her worries, Clay had come over right on time and was in a slightly better mood than last night, although he remained distant and polite. He didn't touch the cinnamon rolls she set out. He didn't say much either, yet they managed to go over all the items Trish had on her to-do list, making sure they were on the same page.

"So, it looks like we'll have a packed house," she said, leaning back, satisfied. "And I can't think of one detail we've forgotten, can you?"

"Nope, you've got it all covered."

"Yeah, on paper it looks good," she agreed, rubbing her hands on her jeans. "But putting it together tomorrow is the real test. I want to go over to Penny's Song as soon as Meggie wakes up to get a mental picture in my head one more time. And make sure the children are ready."

"They'll be ready. Every last one of them is excited about it." Clay took a sip of his coffee.

"And you really think this is going to work?"

"It's brilliant, Trish. I have no doubt."

Trish had doubts about everything in her life lately, but she hoped this gala would raise generous amounts for the charity foundation. She had to put aside her feelings for Clay and deal with her heartache another time. Fortunately, Clay was cooperating, making the Penny's Song gala his top priority, too.

"Well," he said, pushing air out of his lungs, "I've got my own list of things to do, so I'll be going."

He scraped back his chair and rose, putting his hat on.

Trish got up, too, and walked him to the door, grateful their meeting had been a civil affair.

"Oh, I almost forgot." He pulled out a sheet of paper from his pocket. "I had a dinner meeting last night with a contributor who can't make it to the gala. This is our first donation. Thought you'd like to see it." He slipped the paper under her nose.

Trish took a quick look and then looked again. "Fifty thousand dollars!"

The corner of Clay's rigid mouth lifted. "I thought you'd like it."

"Oh my goodness." She clutched her chest, honestly stunned. "Who…how did you…this is amazing!"

"He's an old friend of mine. We had dinner last night and I showed him around Penny's Song. We sat around the campfire, swapping stories with the kids. That's how I know your idea for tomorrow is going to kick some major contributor butt."

"Okay." Trish began to nod, her head bobbing up and down. She couldn't hide her grin. *"Okay."*

She felt better about everything now. Her doubts disappeared, but she hated facing the truth. She'd been just as thrilled that Clay hadn't been with Suzy last night. He'd been with a friend who had deep pockets.

"Trish." Clay's voice was edged with enough intensity to stop her cold.

"What?"

"I think we should display a united front tomorrow, for the sake of Penny's Song."

She agreed instantly. "Of course we will. Our vision has always been on track. At least it's the one thing we have."

He stared at her for a long moment, then finally tipped his hat. "Okay, then I'll see you tomorrow."

It was settled.

Later that day, Trish walked the perimeter of Penny's Song with Meggie and Blake and reminded the children of their part in the gala as she encountered them. One by one, they had given her their reassurances. They knew what to do.

Blake strolled off with Meggie to show her the horses. Trish watched them go, no longer holding her breath, *as tightly,* when Meggie was out of her sight. Her brother wanted to get to know the baby better and Trish thought it a good thing.

She walked up to a rise that overlooked the ranch and peered down, envisioning how it would all come to life tomorrow. After a few minutes, she saw Callie drive into the parking area. When she got out of her car, she spotted Trish and waved, then headed up the hill.

"Hi," she said, immediately noting the baby's absence. "Where's Meggie?"

"Oh, she's down there somewhere." Trish pointed toward the stables. "With my brother."

Callie grinned. "You're making progress."

"Some. I've already called him once."

Callie chuckled, her eyes beaming. "You're bad."

"You think?"

"It's nice that she's spending time with your brother." She paused. "For a second, I was hoping you left the baby with Clay."

"Clay? Uh, no. I haven't done that." Trish shifted her focus back to the ranch below, unable to meet Callie's expectant gaze. She whispered, "It's bad enough that Meggie adores him."

Callie sighed. "And it's terrible that Clay adores Meggie right back."

Trish shot her a glance.

"What? You're not denying that Clay has feelings for Meggie."

"No, I'm not." Sadness swept clear through her. "Not at all. I shouldn't have let it happen. Meggie will miss him terribly when we leave."

"Then don't go." Callie's advice landed like a thud. She made it seem so simple when the whole thing was extremely complicated.

"I have to go. There's nothing keeping me here…anymore. Clay's not…he's not…"

"You know what I think?" Callie said, her voice triumphant. "I think you love Clay and he loves you right back and neither one of you is willing to make the first move. I think you need to forgive him and he needs to forgive you. I think you're only going to be truly happy with each other. The three of you make the perfect family."

Trish was astonished. Callie had put her life into a neat little box, bluntly but honestly. She was right, but Trish couldn't go backward. For once in her life, she wanted to feel truly and completely loved. Nothing had changed between her and Clay. Or had it? She began to doubt herself now and couldn't even formulate her arguments. "But I, no…I can't even…it hurt so much before—"

Callie laid her hand on her arm. "I know. Love hurts. Tagg and I had our share of it, too. But look how happy we are now. What have you got to lose, Trish? You're already set to go home. If it doesn't work out between you and Clay…well, at least you gave your marriage one last valiant effort. I say, go for it."

"But how?"

"Tomorrow. It's your last chance. Dazzle Clay. Make him forget Suzy's name. Do it for Meggie. Do it for Clay. But mostly, do it for you. You deserve it, Trish. You love Clay, don't you?"

Trish held back tears and nodded, closing her eyes.

"Okay, then. Give it one last shot."

When Trish opened her eyes, Callie was smiling, her eyes filled with reassurance.

"Tell me, is Tagg making this same plea to Clay?" Trish asked. "Are you double-teaming us?"

Callie grinned and if Trish was wrong, she might have just put the idea in Callie's head. Her friend narrowed her eyes, shook her head and waved her finger back and forth. "I'll never tell."

Ten

Trish inhaled and took a good look at herself in the bedroom mirror. Tonight she was going for daring times two. She put on a gown made of shimmering silver sequins that clung to her like a tight leather glove. The gown draped low in folds down her back, just above what would be considered indecent. She'd had her hair done in Red Ridge at Beatrice's Salon, styled by Beatrice herself. On one side of her head, a glittery comb pulled her hair severely back only to fill the other side with a mass of long, sweeping blond waves.

Trish turned this way and that gazing critically at herself one last time, wondering if it was all a little too much.

You want sex, Clay had said, the last time she'd dressed up for him. And he'd been right. But this time, much more was at stake. She wanted it all. And if Clay didn't see fit to give it to her, Trish would know right then what her future would look like without him.

"Well, here goes," she said to Meggie.

The baby smiled from her crib, revealing two white buds coming up on her bottom gums. Soon she'd have a mouthful of teeth, but right now those little specks of white looked better than two-carat diamonds.

With Helen's help, she'd dressed the baby in a soft pink ruffled taffeta dress that reached a little below her knees. Her socks were pink, too, and were trimmed with white lace that matched her shoes. Trish put a pink headband bow in her hair and this time, Meggie didn't try to yank it off. The baby seemed to sense something exciting in the air.

"Thanks again for coming with us today," she said as Helen approached the bedroom. "I'm going to need reinforcements with Meggie."

"You've got a lot to do tonight. Don't you worry about Meggie. I'll take great care of her."

"I know you will," Trish said. "And Blake will help, too."

Helen's brown-sugar eyes softened. "You two look pretty enough for a princess ball."

Amused, Trish gave a little chuckle. "I think Meggie would make a great princess. Just look at her, she loves dressing up." Then Trish wrung out her hands. She couldn't stall any longer. She'd spent the entire morning at Penny's Song, running around like a madwoman, bypassing Clay several times, while issuing orders and double checking everything. Now hours later, it was finally time to see this through to the end. "Oh, boy. This is it, isn't it? Time to go?"

Helen came over to lift Meggie out of the crib. "It's time."

A great deal was riding on tonight. Trish prayed for a happy ending. This was her last chance.

Clay parked the car fifty feet from the little ranch and leaned against the hood of his Mercedes for a second, tuxedo jacket slung over his shoulder. Peace and quiet surrounded the land. Not a soul was out. Occasionally, a horse would nicker.

In half an hour Penny's Song would bustle with activity and the ranch would come alive. But right now, the children were bunking down and resting before the activities began and Clay absorbed the silence. A deep sense of pride and honor seeped in and he welcomed it. He knew his father would be proud.

The transformation of Penny's Song from rugged ranch to elegantly appointed gala might have bowled him over if he hadn't been in on Trish's plan from the very beginning. It was all going to start a little before sundown. There was nothing like sunset at Red Ridge. Even the weather was cooperating. Cooling easterly breezes, enough to ruffle your hair and lift your shirt, freshened the air. Soon the horizon would burst forth in an orange-red haze, forming a shimmering halo atop the crimson mountains beyond.

Fancy tables with white linens and clear flower-filled glass boots sat front and center on the widest part of the street between the bunkhouse and general store. The tables were supported underneath by a vast wooden floor. When the sun set, twinkle lights would blink on and fill the entire little ranch with wonder and awe, but first Trish wanted Penny's Song to be seen as is, in glorious fading daylight.

Air whooshed out of Clay's lungs in a deep pensive sigh. Tagg's parting shot in the stables today stuck in his head and only now, while he was engulfed in peace, did he give the statement credence. "Don't be an ass. If you have any doubt in your mind, don't let them go."

Clay didn't want to hear it. He'd blocked out his brother's comments. But in the end, it hadn't helped. He'd been saying the same thing to himself for the past week.

Don't let them go.

Wes appeared on the street, then Preston and Suzy and several others from the medical volunteer team. The kids came out of the bunkhouse, one at time, meandering, looking at the set tables and decorations that Trish had arranged. Their excited faces were just one more layer of pride to add to his thick skin. Clay met some of the kids, showed them around and told them to just be themselves when meeting the visitors.

"This is exciting, Clay," Suzy said, her eyes glowing. "You clean up real nice. The tux looks great on you."

Clay pulled at his bola tie and sent her a crooked smile. He was ordered to wear it by Trish. She'd been right, wearing black tie gave the gala the elegant contrast it needed against the backdrop of pasture smells and dirt underfoot. "You do, too. Pretty dress."

Suzy sent him a dazzling smile. "Thank you."

"The place looks amazing," Wes remarked as he strode by.

Heath, an eleven-year-old boy with a knack for grooming horses, ran up to him and announced, "Mr. Worth, I like those boots on the tables!"

"Hey, yeah. Pretty cool," Preston added, putting a hand on Heath's shoulder.

"I had nothing to do with it," Clay said with a wink. "You can tell Mrs. Worth when she arrives."

Everyone got busy and Clay walked over to the saloon to speak with the catering chef. When he came out, Penny's Song was starting to buzz. The gates to the ranch had opened ten minutes ago and a small crowd of people were approaching after parking their cars and trucks in a cleared field. Several limousines pulled up, along with town cars.

He stood in the middle of it all looking on, sheltering a hollow ache in the pit of his stomach. He hadn't done this alone. This vision had been Trish's, too, and she'd made this evening come alive. He searched the grounds for her, wanting to see her reaction, wanting to share this with her.

And then he spotted her.

She'd parked her Volvo behind the east corral, in a special section closer to the ranch than the other parking areas. He watched her lift Meggie into her arms. The baby clung on, her bright eyes absorbing the scene, a bundle of pink fluff against Trish's radiant silver gown. His wife's honey-blond hair was swept to one side of her head, spilling into a soft caress on her shoulder. The shimmery dress she wore hung on to her body for dear life.

The two stood there for a moment, mother and daughter, each of them stunning in their own way. Each of them filling up the hole in his heart.

A shudder ran through his body and made him twitch. Clay's stomach roiled and pitched like a boat adrift in the perfect storm. He staggered, physically moved by the reaction. There wasn't anything he could do but stand there, try to keep his balance and watch them. Smacked with a wall of reality, his breathing went shallow.

Trish and Meggie *belonged* with him.

They were his family.

He'd known it for days now but refused to face the truth. Tagg had been right. He couldn't let them leave.

Hell of a time to discover it. The crowd was swarming in now and he had an agenda to follow. His boots hit the path and he headed their way. By the time he'd reached them, Helen had Meggie in the stroller and Blake had stepped up. Jackson, Callie and Tagg joined them and he was surrounded by his clan, offering congratulations and pats on the back.

Trish had a wide smile for him, her eyes incredibly blue with excitement. "Look at it, Clay. It's working. The kids, they're interacting with the guests. They're showing them the ropes and the adults are eating it up."

It was true. Already the children and volunteers were gathered in little groups, showing the early arriving guests what they'd learned, doing mini demonstrations and giving out tokens. Trish had "adult" gifts ready in the general store for the guests. But they had to earn their tokens first by visiting certain areas of the ranch and in some instances, partaking in events.

"Yeah, your hard work is paying off."

"Not just me," she said. "Everyone has worked hard at Penny's Song. I only put this evening together. The rest of them keep it running all week long."

He strode alongside her and the others as they chattered about Penny's Song, pointing out locals they knew or children they'd met this week. Even Meggie was enthralled.

Clay cursed his bad timing. All he wanted to do right now was tell Trish she looked gorgeous. He wanted to hold her in his arms. He wanted to ask her to stay.

They reached the center of town and Clay got her alone for a second, away from Blake, Helen and the baby. He stared into her eyes. "I need to talk to you tonight. After the gala. I'll come by the house."

Trish's mouth rounded to a silent *O*. Then her eyes darted away quickly. "I know. We have to talk." Resignation rang in her voice, but before Clay could explain that it wasn't about the divorce, a hearty slap to his back brought him up short. Annoyed, he turned, recognizing Harold Overton, a big-time oilman from Texas, smiling at him. "Hey, Clay, how're you doing?"

"Fine, Harold. Good to see you here." Clay shook the man's hand.

"I flew up from Houston just because you asked."

"I appreciate that."

"I'd like to see this place firsthand."

"Sure, sure. But first, let me introduce you to—" Clay spun around but Trish was no longer by his side. She'd been whisked away by three local women who were yakking nonstop.

"Never mind. My coconspirator of this foundation is busy at the moment. Let me show you around." Clay led the head honcho of the Houston Livestock Show and Rodeo on a personal tour of the facility.

It was like that most of the evening, Trish and Clay barely getting in a few words together before one of them was taken away to tend to business or some minor crisis on the grounds.

The Ridgecrest Resort Hotel staff served appetizers on silver platters as day lent itself to night. Slowly the guests took their seats as pinpoints of light lit the entire area. Rumor had it Trish had commissioned ten thousand twinkling lights to be strung up to shower the little ranch with illumination. They were everywhere, draped along the corral fences, outlining the outer buildings and wrapped around the bases and branches of the trees. Penny's Song sparkled from the ground up.

The daytime bustling ebbed to a subtle hum of voices. And before dinner, Clay found Trish and escorted her toward the podium set in front of the general store. It was the first time he'd touched her tonight. His hand was gentle on her bare back, though a possessive wave of pride filled his chest. Then he wound his hand around her waist splaying his fingers over her hip and brought her closer as they walked side by side to greet their guests.

"I want to thank you all for coming," he began, speaking into a microphone. "Hopefully, the last hour has shown you a little bit of what we do here at Penny's Song. My wife, Trish," Clay said without pause, noting her slide him a sideways glance, "is partially responsible for the idea behind our facility, but she gets full credit for tonight's gala. This was all her idea. Are you having fun?"

Applause broke out and Clay nodded his approval. Trish beamed. "Now, I'll let Trish say a few words."

Trish took the mic and spoke a little about her brother,

Blake, and then relayed stories about the other special children she'd met at the facility. She explained how working here these past few weeks had enriched her life. How this aspect of recovery, trying to filter children back into society, had been overlooked up until now and how Trish hoped that more and more facilities like Penny's Song might be developed.

Clay took over from there, introducing a few parents whose children had benefited from Penny's Song and their testimonials were short and sweet.

"I hope after dinner, you all stay for campfire songs over by the corrals. We've got bleachers and chairs set up. Maybe indulge in s'mores and roasted nuts."

And later, once the meal was over, a big, crackling fire was built in the clearing. The adults gathered around as the children taught them campfire songs. Everyone had smiles on their faces and it did Clay's heart good to see how well the gala had turned out.

After the campfire, Clay stood alone by the stables watching the guests depart. One hundred contributors had written checks to keep Penny's Song afloat for the year. With Worth backing as well, Clay had no doubt they'd do fine. But his mind wasn't solely on fundraising tonight. It was on Trish and what he'd say to her. How he'd formulate the words when he went over to the guesthouse to pour out his heart.

Deep in thought, he didn't hear Suzy approach, crying hysterically, until she was inches from his face.

"It's my father, Clay. It's bad. It's bad." The panic in her voice woke him out of his stupor. "He's had a heart attack," she cried. Makeup-smeared tears spilled down her cheeks and smudged her face. Desperately, the words tumbled out in a rush. "I just got the message. They've been trying to reach me for an hour. They say he's barely holding on. I should get there quickly. Oh God, Clay. Oh God, what am I going to do?"

Clay wrapped her in his arms and shushed her crying. He scanned the area, for a second, but the cleanup crew had come in to break things down and the grounds were in chaos. He couldn't find Trish or anyone else he recognized. He hugged Suzy to him and began walking to his car. "Don't worry, Suze. It's gonna be all right. I'll take you to him right now."

Clay ran his hands down his face. Day-old stubble lay underneath his palms, but he didn't give a damn. His head, though, hurt like a sonofabitch and he wished to high heaven the throbbing would die down. He'd been awake for twenty-eight hours straight, having gone with Suzy when her father was airlifted to Phoenix last night. Once back home, he'd settled Suzy down and tucked her into bed, then drove to the guesthouse at breakneck speed. Trish hadn't answered her phone all night.

He knocked at the door, impatient. "Trish."

Thankfully, he heard footsteps approach. A deep sigh of relief escaped and even though it wouldn't be the flowery confession he'd planned, she was here and they could talk.

The door opened and his mouth dipped into a frown. "Blake."

"Hello, Clay."

Clay craned his head past Blake to look inside the house. "I'm here for Trish. Is she home?"

Blake's expression faltered and he drove a sharp breath into his lungs. "No, she's not here."

"Where did she go?"

Blake's eyes softened with sympathy and an uneasy feeling poked Clay in the gut. "She went home. Back to Nashville."

"What?" Clay rocked back on his heels. He had trouble controlling the pitch in his voice. "Already? She wasn't due to leave until tomorrow."

"I know. Come in, Clay. Have a seat. We need to talk."

Clay strode past Blake and refused his offer to sit down. "Why the hell did she leave early? And why are you here?"

"I'll answer the second question first. I'm here because I owe it to my sister. I'm here because I knew eventually you'd show up and you need to hear a few things about Trish."

"What do I need to hear? She couldn't wait to get out of here," Clay said angrily, but he wasn't sure who deserved his wrath more, him or her. He'd been too late and now his wife was gone. He felt the loss immediately in the pit of his stomach.

Blake didn't disagree. "Yes, that's true. She left very early this morning."

"Well, hell."

"Yeah, she's been through that, too."

Clay snapped his head up and stared at Blake. "What does that mean? How has she been through hell?"

"Sit yourself down." This time it was an order. "I'll get us some coffee and then I'll explain."

Clay didn't have it in him to argue. He was still trying to deal with Trish leaving the ranch. Meggie was gone, too. He squeezed his eyes shut. Damn. Damn. Damn. They were both gone, out of his life. He sat on the sofa and when Blake shoved a cup of coffee onto the glass table, he grabbed it and took a gulp.

Blake took a seat in a chair that faced him. "She saw you leave with Suzy last night."

Clay shook his head quickly and the pain was like a knife twisting in his skull. "It's not what you think. Suzy's dad had a heart attack. I took her to the hospital. He was critical and needed the best medical attention. He was airlifted to Phoenix. Suzy was hysterical and begged me not to leave her alone. I went with her. And I'm glad I did because her father died last night. He was a friend, Blake. And I had a choice to make. I couldn't leave Suzy's side, but I called Trish the very second I could to explain. She didn't pick up. I left several phone messages last night."

"My sister said you wanted to talk to her after the gala. Then she saw you taking off with Suzy. She was very upset and too heartbroken to listen to your excuses. Her words, not mine. She figured the marriage was over and you'd made your choice. She was really hurt, Clay. I couldn't talk her out of leaving this morning."

Blake walked over to a side table, bringing back a stack of papers. "And she signed these."

He handed them over. Clay didn't have to look at them to know they were the final divorce papers. He rubbed his forehead, his thumb and forefingers pulling tight the skin there. He let go a few choice curses and then looked at Blake. "I don't want this."

"I figured as much. But you have to understand about Trish. She was always the one getting dumped on in our household. I was ill for most of my childhood, but Trish was the one who paid the higher price. She was never put first. My parents catered to me. They had to, to keep me alive. They spent all their spare time with me, taking me to specialists, keeping me company during my hospital stays, giving me attention when they thought I was depressed. They had no time for Trish. And I saw it happening, but I was too young to realize how it would affect my sister later.

"She was reliable and independent and my parents thought that she didn't need them. They never were there for her, Clay. Not for school functions. Not for shopping dates. There were never any mother/daughter things. Trish had been forced to grow up fast. And she feared becoming a mother and making those same mistakes. She feared not being good enough. She didn't want to injure a child the same way she'd been injured. By neglect. She held on to her independence as a crutch, yes, but more so, to keep from getting hurt. It's the way my sister defends herself."

Clay's muddled brain filed the information away. "That's why she leaves?"

"I think so," Blake said. "She wants someone to put her first, Clay. That's all she's ever wanted. To be blunt, you didn't make much of an effort to get her back the last time. And then you sent the divorce papers. It really broke her up."

"Damn it." He ran his hands through his hair, pulling the strands taut. He blew out a breath, letting everything sink in. He saw Trish more clearly now and the mistakes he'd made with her. "Okay, I get that."

"Good. Then I'll be on my way."

"Thanks." Clay rose from the sofa to shake Blake's hand. "I appreciate your staying to explain."

"You're welcome." Blake studied him with narrowed eyes and gave a shake of the head. "You should get some sleep, Clay. You look like hell."

He didn't know where it came from, but laughter escaped and the release of tension felt damn good. "Do me a favor. Don't say anything about this conversation to Trish. I need to explain everything to her myself. I need to apologize. In person."

"You got it."

"You're a good brother, Blake."

He nodded before he reached the front door. "Be sure to remind Trish of that when you see her."

Toss out unnecessary junk. Check.
Pack up your collectibles. Check.
Call the Realtor. Check.
Stop thinking about Clay...

Trish sat in her kitchen and stared at the list on the table. That last box to check off wasn't written down on paper but was on her mind constantly. She had a mental check-off list that included *Don't Be Too Stupid to Live, Don't Look Back* and *Stop Crying* among others, but so far, Trish hadn't been able to put a check mark in any of those boxes.

Worse yet, she feared she'd hurt Meggie by allowing her to get close to Clay. She wondered if the baby felt the loss.

As much as you do.

The gala had been the highlight of her life, both professionally and personally. She'd felt a deep sense of community with the patrons that night and with the children who'd been so eager to show off what they'd learned and by doing so, they'd also shown everyone how far they'd come. People seemed to enjoy themselves.

Donations had come flooding in once the benefactors realized that the smaller scope of the facility was exactly what made it work so well. She'd wanted townsfolk as well as the big-money donors to see the Worth charity not as an ostentatious foundation but one that really touched hearts and minds.

The problem was her heart and mind had been severely shaken that night. From a distance, she'd seen Suzy snuggled up against Clay's chest and being huddled off into his car and only the worst-case scenarios played in her head. Clay and Suzy had plans to celebrate the gala's success on their own. They couldn't wait to be together. Trish had done her part for Penny's Song and he was through with her. She'd served her purpose. Clay hadn't even stuck around until the very end.

Like a dope, Trish had held out hope for their marriage. But seeing him leave with Suzy had been the last straw. Her heart torn to shreds, she couldn't stay in Red Ridge any longer. There was no sense in prolonging the divorce. It was what Clay wanted all along. She'd been a fool to think she could dazzle him and make her marriage work.

It was a painful pill to swallow.

Her tears were like an automatic faucet. As soon as she

thought of Clay, they'd spill down her cheeks. She hated her weakness. She hated the feeling of failure, yet again. She had to be strong for Meggie's sake, but inside she was completely shattered.

She wiped her face with her sleeve and sniffled. Taking a deep breath, she grabbed a sheet from a stack of unfolded newspapers and picked up one of her Waterford crystal wine goblets. "Don't think I'm going to need any of these for a while."

Meggie sat in the high chair beside the table and looked on, fascinated by the sound of paper crinkling as Trish positioned the glass on the sheet and rolled it until the goblet had disappeared into newspaper print. She set the wrapped glass into a square box labeled "Kitchen" and then started on the next one.

There was a knock at her door and Meggie turned to the sound. "That'll be your aunt Jodi," she explained to the baby. "She's coming to help us pack."

Trish was grateful for the company. Her assistant was a godsend. They'd been cooped up in her apartment for two days. It was time to start living again.

When she opened the door, she froze. A dozen thoughts entered her head, but she could only concentrate on one. "What are you doing here?"

Dark brows lifted at her sassy tone. Clay didn't answer. Instead he strode past her and entered the room without invitation. He held a manila folder in one hand and then whipped off his hat with the other as he took in her tiny apartment. He glanced at Meggie and the darkest rims of his eyes brightened for a second.

Meggie practically burst out of her high chair when she saw him. Trish was furious. He couldn't just show up here unannounced. He couldn't come in and out of her life this way.

She ignored Meggie's reaction and prayed the baby wouldn't cry for him.

"I asked you a question, Clay. What are you doing here?"

He opened the folder and pointed at the papers inside. Trish recognized them immediately as the signed divorce papers she'd left for him. "You *do* know that I'm a very wealthy man."

Trish took a swallow. She nodded.

"My part of Worth Ranch is worth millions, not to mention the wad of dough I made before that on the music circuit."

Trish knew what he was worth. And he knew that she knew. "So?"

Clay glanced at the half-packed box on the table and the few other boxes sitting on the floor. Her new home wouldn't close escrow for weeks, but Trish had wanted to get a head start before the actual move.

He strolled around the room, taking it in and keeping her waiting. Her nerves jumped as he stopped by the kitchen window to look out. His presence filled the small area and it drove her crazy, his casual meandering. When he walked over to the high chair, all of the breath she held whooshed out.

Don't pick Meggie up, Clay. Don't make her want you.

Clay stroked Meggie's head. Her tiny curls sprung up under his fingertips. Then he bent to kiss the very top of her head. It was the gentlest, sweetest kiss on earth.

Trish's heart couldn't break any more. There was nothing left to splinter.

Clay tossed the folder down on the table, his gaze pinned to hers. He moved toward her and with each step he took, her body trembled more and more. When he finally faced her, they stood inches apart and his voice broke the deafening silence. "So," he began, "why is it you ask nothing of me? And I want to give you the world."

Her eyes drifted closed. She didn't just hear that. He didn't just say he wanted to give her the world. Was that financially, because he felt sorry for Meggie? "I…don't understand."

Clay smiled, a widespread, eye-crinkling, beaming, megawatt smile. "I know you don't. That's our problem, you don't understand me and I don't understand you. But I love you, Trish. I love you and the baby. It's the one thing I truly understand."

She couldn't believe her ears. He sounded sincere. And she wanted to believe him, but there was Suzy. There was *always* Suzy. "You stood me up. To be with Suzy. I saw you leave the gala with her."

He winced. "I know and I'm very sorry about that. I wanted to be with you that night, Trish. You have to believe me. I'd planned to come over and ask you to stay with me, but Suzy's dad had a heart attack. He died and she was inconsolable."

Clay explained the circumstances of that night and all Trish could do was listen to him plead his case. "I never wanted you to think you didn't matter to me. If I could do it all over again, I would have found you first, to explain where I was going. I'm sorry I made you doubt me."

Trish saw the unabashed truth in his eyes. Then she thought of Suzy and what it must have been like for her, losing her father that way. "Is Suzy all right?"

"She will be. She's strong. And it's time she realized that. I told her I was coming here. I told her how much I love you. Suzy and I…it was never real between us and she knows that now. I had to come for you, Trish. You belong with me. You're the most important person in my life."

"Oh, wow." It was the moment she'd secretly prayed for, to hear Clay say that and really mean it. Clay had come for her. He'd made the effort to seek her out and apologize. This was the white-knight moment she thought would never happen for her.

He went on, "I let my friendship with Suzy get in the way of our marriage and that won't happen again. I had one woman who relied on me too much and then I had you... who never relied on me for anything. You never gave me your trust, Trish. I need that. You need to know that I'd move heaven and earth for you and Meggie. I won't fail you."

Trish wrestled with the hope that overwhelmed her. She wanted to believe him. "Suzy seemed like the perfect woman for you. That's why I couldn't stand her being around. She was everything I wasn't."

Clay took her into his arms. He held her firmly, his grip wrapping around her as if to say he won't ever let go. His eyes softened and he spoke with dire conviction. "I'm *looking* at the perfect woman for me. There's not a doubt in my mind."

"Really?"

He smiled again—a dazzler—and her heart burst with joy. "I should have never pressured you about having a baby. I guess I couldn't understand why you kept denying me, but I get it now. Your brother made me see what I couldn't grasp before. I'm sorry, Trish, for all you've gone through." His head began shaking as he continued, "You deserve so much, the best. And I want to give that to you. I hope you can forgive me for being thickheaded."

Trish steadied her out-of-control breathing. She paused for a few moments and then nodded. "Yes, yes, I can forgive you, if you can forgive me for walking out on you. I shouldn't have. I should have confronted you and gotten the truth."

"That would've been nice," he said guilelessly.

"I'm sorry, Clay." She meant it from the bottom of her heart.

Clay's lips twisted. "I was an ass."

Trish threw her head back and laughed. Meggie chimed in

with infectious cackles that filled the entire apartment with sweetness. "You're forgiven."

His dark eyes gleamed with so much hope that Trish wanted to pinch herself to make sure all of this was real. Clay had come for her. He'd put her first. He really loved her. "I will spend my entire life making you happy. I'll do whatever it takes and that's a promise. So are we good, sweetheart? Can I burn those damn divorce papers?"

She smiled. "I'll light the match." There was no doubt left in her mind. "We are *so* good."

Clay sighed with relief and wrapped her in his arms. His lips came down on hers again in a lighter kiss and he poured his heart out to her with three simple words she'd never tire of hearing. "I love you."

"I love you, too."

But then a thought struck and she nibbled on her lower lip, hesitating.

"What is it?" he asked, ducking his head to level a gaze at her.

She hated to bring this up, but the air needed clearing. "There's still my career to think about and the house I just bought."

Clay only smiled at her, his expression earnest. "I never expected you to give up your work, Trish. Maybe you thought you had to, to be a good mother, but—"

"No, I've been thinking about it," she said softly. "I want to be with Meggie as much as I can. And spend time at Penny's Song. Jodi has been hinting about a partnership. Maybe it's time for me to let go a little. I can do that."

"Whatever you decide is fine. We'll work it out. And if you love the house, we'll keep it and spend time here in Nashville if you want. I don't care. As long as we're together."

That's exactly how she felt. She wanted to be with Clay. She wanted the three of them to be a family. All the other things *would* work themselves out. "Oh, wow. It's so liberating."

"What is?" Clay asked with a big smile.

"Letting go." Trish felt a great weight lift from her shoulders. She could finally breathe again. She could finally see a future that wasn't all planned out before her, one that might take twists and turns. And that was okay. Everything was going to be all right.

He walked over to Meggie and unfastened the strap on her high chair to lift her out. Trish stood beside him as Meggie wrapped her arms around Clay's neck and cuddled his chest. He held her tight and breathed in her precious baby smells. There was no doubt they loved each other.

Clay met her gaze over the baby's head. "Trust me?"

"I do." And she really meant it.

"Save your *I do's* until we get back to the ranch."

"Why?"

A teasing glint entered his eyes. "You'll both have to wait and see."

Trish sent him a dubious look. What was he up to?

"You trust me, remember?"

And suddenly Trish wasn't sure that was wise.

They stood on the bank of Elizabeth Lake just before the sun set beyond Red Ridge Mountains. The sky screamed with an eruption of pink-orange hues and the air held on to its last breath of warmth.

The Worth clan—Jackson, Tagg and Callie—along with Wes and Helen looked on as Clay spoke vows straight from his heart to his wife and child. It was right to do this here, in the place where every Worth man had proposed marriage to his bride since the ranch was founded.

Trish, in turn, spoke her vows, too, renewing the love they shared, including Meggie in her pledge as his newly adopted daughter. Clay had never felt so proud and honored and he choked up a little when it came time to seal their marriage vows.

Tagg handed him the ring box made of fine black velvet. Clay opened it and nimbly lifted out the ruby-and-diamond ring he'd had made for Trish over a year ago. He slid it carefully onto her finger. "To the woman I love most in the world, my wife."

Trish gasped and held back tears as she looked lovingly at the ring he'd put on her finger. Her voice trembled when she spoke. "I love you, Clay. I will be the mother to your children and I will love *us* forever."

Clay felt himself beaming inside. They were a family.

Next, he was handed another box, this one made of carved leather, weathered and old. It held the family legacy, the ruby necklace that had been in his family for generations. It had once belonged to the namesake of the very body of water and land they stood upon, his great-grandmother many times over, Lizzie Worth.

With trembling fingers, he lifted the necklace out, the gold catching the last of the day's light and the pear-shaped ruby meant only for the first Worth heir. It was to be handed down from one generation to the other. "To the other woman I love most in the world, my daughter, Meggie."

With intense pride, Clay put the ruby necklace around Meggie's chubby throat and secured the clasp. The pear-shaped gem shone as rosy and beautiful as his baby's cheeks. He kissed both wife and child softly, the power of his love too strong to say with words alone. But Trish knew. And so did Meggie.

The three of them were a pretty little picture.

Clay had no doubt.

* * * * *

PASSION

For a spicier, decidedly hotter read—
this is your destination for romance!

COMING NEXT MONTH
AVAILABLE JANUARY 10, 2012

#2131 TERMS OF ENGAGEMENT
Ann Major

#2132 SEX, LIES AND THE SOUTHERN BELLE
Dynasties: The Kincaids
Kathie DeNosky

#2133 THE NANNY BOMBSHELL
Billionaires and Babies
Michelle Celmer

#2134 A COWBOY COMES HOME
Colorado Cattle Barons
Barbara Dunlop

#2135 INTO HIS PRIVATE DOMAIN
The Men of Wolff Mountain
Janice Maynard

#2136 A SECRET BIRTHRIGHT
Olivia Gates

You can find more information on upcoming Harlequin® titles,
free excerpts and more at www.HarlequinInsideRomance.com.

*Brittany Grayson survived a horrible ordeal at the hands
of a serial killer known as The Professional...
who's after her now?*

*Harlequin® Romantic Suspense presents a new installment
in Carla Cassidy's reader-favorite miniseries,*
LAWMEN OF BLACK ROCK.

Enjoy a sneak peek of
TOOL BELT DEFENDER.

*Available January 2012
from Harlequin® Romantic Suspense.*

"**B**rittany?" His voice was deep and pleasant and made
her realize she'd been staring at him openmouthed through
the screen door.

"Yes, I'm Brittany and you must be..." Her mind suddenly went blank.

"Alex. Alex Crawford, Chad's friend. You called him
about a deck?"

As she unlocked the screen, she realized she wasn't
quite ready yet to allow a stranger inside, especially a male
stranger.

"Yes, I did. It's nice to meet you, Alex. Let's walk around
back and I'll show you what I have in mind," she said. She
frowned as she realized there was no car in her driveway.
"Did you walk here?" she asked.

His eyes were a warm blue that stood out against his
tanned face and was complemented by his slightly shaggy
dark hair. "I live three doors up." He pointed up the street to
the Walker home that had been on the market for a while.

"How long have you lived there?"

"I moved in about six weeks ago," he replied as they

walked around the side of the house.

That explained why she didn't know the Walkers had moved out and Mr. Hard Body had moved in. Six weeks ago she'd still been living at her brother Benjamin's house trying to heal from the trauma she'd lived through.

As they reached the backyard she motioned toward the broken brick patio just outside the back door. "What I'd like is a wooden deck big enough to hold a barbecue pit and an umbrella table and, of course, lots of people."

He nodded and pulled a tape measure from his tool belt. "An outdoor entertainment area," he said.

"Exactly," she replied and watched as he began to walk the site. The last thing Brittany had wanted to think about over the past eight months of her life was men. But looking at Alex Crawford definitely gave her a slight flutter of pure feminine pleasure.

Will Brittany be able to heal in the arms of Alex,
her hotter-than-sin handyman...or will a second
psychopath silence her forever? Find out in
TOOL BELT DEFENDER
Available January 2012
from Harlequin® Romantic Suspense
wherever books are sold.